Emily stood on the sidewalk in front of David's loft

Should she go up or not? She really did feel that he was a true soul mate. But what if he was entertaining another woman? Ignoring the flurry of jealousy, Emily told herself that it would be good for David to start dating. Maybe, then, someday soon, he'd wake up and realize that Liza wasn't worth his love and adoration.

Meanwhile, six blocks away, David's foot hit the brakes even before his mind registered that he was practically at Emily's front door. Her lights were on. She must be home. What if she was home with a date? A funny feeling came over him even as he told himself he approved. After all, he did believe that Chris wasn't worthy of Emily's devotion.

Dear Reader,

It's amazing to believe, but Temptation is ten years old this month and we are celebrating in a big way!

We wanted you to share in our festivities so you will see that each of our glorious new raspberry-coloured covers carries a special 10th Anniversary balloon. We have also pulled out the stops with our selection of books this month—each one a special tempting treat—and the temptation continues over the next few months as we bring you a new mini-series about **love lost…love found**. Look out for JoAnn Ross's **Lost Loves** novel *The Return of Caine O'Halloran* in March.

Whether you are a long-standing or new reader of Temptation, we hope you will continue to enjoy the books we have lined up for you.

After ten tempting years, *nobody* can resist

YOU WERE MEANT FOR ME

BY

ELISE TITLE

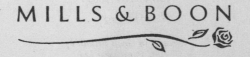

MILLS & BOON

*MILLS & BOON and the Rose Device are trademarks of the
publisher.
TEMPTATION is a trademark of Harlequin Enterprises Limited, used
under licence.
This edition published by arrangement with Harlequin Enterprises
B.V.
First published in Great Britain in 1995
by Harlequin Mills & Boon Limited, Eton House, 18-24 Paradise
Road,
Richmond, Surrey TW9 1SR*

© Elise Title 1993

ISBN 0 263 79065 7

21 - 9502

*Printed in Great Britain by
BPC Paperbacks Ltd*

Prologue

Emily at Twelve

DAWN POKED EMILY, who almost choked on a kernel of popcorn.

"Quit it," Emily muttered. "This is the best part."

"Wanna bet?"

An older couple sitting behind the two girls in the darkened movie theater, shushed them.

Dawn poked Emily again. "It's your boyfriend."

Emily's gaze darted to Chris Anders. The blond-haired, blue-eyed high-school star quarterback was sauntering down the aisle with two buddies. All three were wearing their red-and-yellow team jackets.

Immediately, Emily ditched her glasses, then sat up straight.

"I *knew* you still liked him," Dawn said knowingly.

Emily frowned. Why had she ever been dumb enough to have confided in Dawn that she'd had a crush on Chris since she was in the second grade?

"I do not," Emily retorted. "Anyway, he thinks I'm just a kid." If he thought of her at all.

He was almost at their row. Emily shut her eyes and prayed. And wished she was wearing something other than a baggy T-shirt and even baggier jeans. She looked like a slob. She looked as fat as a house. She looked . . .

Chris stopped in the aisle, glancing in her direction. Emily's breath stopped.

Dawn poked her again as the three boys made their way along their row.

Emily thought she just might die when Chris actually slouched into the seat right beside her, his pals sitting down next to him.

"Hey, great seats," he drawled to his friends. Even though Chris had moved from South Carolina to Connecticut back when he was in the fifth grade, he still had a faint Southern accent that Emily absolutely adored.

His two buddies chuckled.

"Hey, Em."

Emily couldn't believe her ears. Chris Anders, the gorgeous hunk of Groton High, greeting her! By name. Better still, by her nickname. Emily could only nod. Her mouth felt like it was filled with glue instead of saliva.

"How's the movie?" he whispered.

Oh my God, he's having a conversation with me. I must be dreaming. If I am, don't let me wake up.

She cleared her throat. "Okay. I guess," she whispered back. Actually it was her favorite movie. She'd already seen it three times. It was one of those soppy tearjerkers and she didn't want Chris to think she wasn't cool.

Dawn giggled. Emily poked her. Really, Dawn could be so immature.

The boy next to Chris whispered something to him. Out of the corner of her eye, Emily saw Chris grin. He was still grinning when he looked over at her again.

Emily's heart was racing as she smiled back—a small smile, to conceal her braces.

Without even asking, he dipped his hand into her container of popcorn and helped himself to a handful. Emily was ecstatic. Why, it was almost as if they were . . . on a date!

He popped a few kernels in his mouth, winked a[nd] whispered, "I'm crazy about the stuff."

"Me, too." Which was a lie. The kernels were alwa[ys get]ting stuck in her braces. She had sworn off candy becau[se her] face had started to break out. "Here, have some...." S[he] started to pass the popcorn to Chris just as he leaned f[or]ward in his seat. The container tipped, the popcorn spillin[g] out on his lap. And it was buttered!

Emily was mortified. She wanted to die right there on the spot. That wasn't even the worst of it. Suddenly a girl sitting in the row in front of her—in the seat directly in front of Chris's—turned around and laughed. Chris scooped up some of the popcorn from his lap and playfully tossed it at her.

"You'll be sorry," he teased the blond-haired girl whom Emily now recognized as Julie Reed, the prettiest and most popular girl at Groton High.

Just before Chris climbed over the seat to the vacant one beside Julie, he gave Emily one of his heartthrob smiles. "Thanks, kid. I owe you."

At the end of the movie tears streamed down Emily's cheeks, but they had nothing to do with what was on the screen.

David at Sixteen

"YOU REALLY ARE a lifesaver, David," Liza said, giving him a peck on the cheek. "I'm lousy with figures."

David smiled wryly as he packed away his algebra book. "Oh, I don't know about that."

Liza ruffled his short brown hair. "You're cute." She plucked off his glasses. "And so smart, it makes me sick." Playfully, she tossed a notebook at him.

"Okay," he conceded, ducking. "I am smart."

Liza sprawled out on her bed.

losed door. "Doesn't your mom

Why, you're like my kid brother."

I happen to be six months older than

to her stomach, chin propped in her hands,
a scrutinizing look as he put his tortoiseshell-
glasses back on.

u know something, David. You could be cute if you put
ome effort into it. You're tall and you've got nice green eyes —
you ought to think about wearing contacts. And working out
in a gym. And getting your hair cut by a stylist instead of that
awful barber who practically shaves your head."

"When we were in elementary school, you used to call me
Nerdo, remember?"

Liza sighed dramatically, her gaze moving from David to
the full-length mirror across the room. "Well, we've both
improved since grade school. Thank goodness."

"You've always looked great," David said softly, taking in
Liza's long dark silky hair, her striking violet eyes, her slender body that curved in all the right places. He'd had a crush
on her since third grade when he'd kissed her in the school
play—even though she'd put up an awful stink about the kiss
to their teacher, Mrs. Moynihan.

Liza dragged her gaze away from her reflection. "Are you
going to the dance on Saturday night?"

David's mouth went dry. He'd been trying to build up the
courage all evening to ask Liza to go with him to the dance,
knowing that she'd broken up with her latest boyfriend that
very afternoon—one in a long string. Liza had been "in love"
more often than most people ate cold cereal for breakfast.
David figured his number had to come up one of these days.
Maybe this was the day.

He readjusted his glasses. "I don't have a date yet, if that's what you're asking."

She beamed at him. "Guess what, kiddo. You do now."

David stared at her in astonishment, his palms sweaty, his pulse racing. He couldn't believe his ears. Liza was going to the dance with him. How many times had he dreamed of this? As many times as there had been dances. His mind went into overdrive. Could he get fitted for contact lenses in time? Could he get an appointment with a hair stylist? Was it possible to bulk up at the gym in five days?

With an enormous effort, he located his voice. "That's . . . great."

Liza grabbed for the phone and started to dial.

"Who're you calling?" David asked, puzzled.

"My friend, Jen Baker from Palo Alto. She's visiting her grandparents here in Berkeley for the week. We were best friends at camp for four summers."

David was beside himself. Could Liza be so excited about going to a dance with him that she couldn't wait to let her best friend know? Wait until he got home and started phoning his buddies. They were never going to believe him.

"Jen? It's me. Liza. Guess what?" she said, winking at David. "You've got yourself a date for the dance."

David's heart sank. Shot down even before he'd had a few minutes to enjoy the fantasy.

"Yes, Jen. I'm looking at him right now. He's adorable. You're gonna love him."

David smiled wanly, but felt like crying. Maybe if he'd gotten those contact lenses a lot sooner . . .

Emily at Nineteen

EMILY DASHED across the campus, her auburn hair slapping against her cheeks. When she got to the quadrangle, she pulled her wool jacket closed, hoisted her large leather pouch higher up on her shoulder and bounced down the concrete steps that led to the university infirmary.

Chris was in one of the few private rooms reserved for VIP students. You couldn't get much more VIP than star quarterback of the Michigan Muskrats.

"Hi," she said breezily, glancing from Chris's face to the cast encasing his leg. "How's it going?"

"Em, am I glad to see you." Over the years, instead of losing his Southern drawl, Chris had learned to capitalize on it. Emily wasn't the only woman who found it sexy.

She brightened at his warm, almost-desperately-happy-to-see-her greeting. Ever since he'd busted his leg in the Ohio game, she'd felt that he took her daily Florence Nightingale visits for granted. Didn't he know that she often lay awake in bed at night fantasizing what it would be like to nurse him back to health—not here in a public place like the school infirmary with doctors, nurses, buddies, and especially his league of female fans constantly popping in and out, but in a cozy private cabin far away in the wilderness? Just the two of them before a roaring fire, on a bearskin rug, Chris telling her in that wonderful Southern drawl how much she meant to him, wanting her even more than she wanted him, the two of them coming up with endlessly creative ways to make love despite his cast. . . .

"Your face is kind of red. Is it cold outside?"

Emily nodded, then dug her hand into her pouch, pulling out a double burger and a large bag of greasy fries—the goodies only slightly cooled off, thanks to her hundred-yard dash from the fast-food shop.

Chris snatched up his bounty with less gusto than usual. "Thanks, darlin'."

She gave him a close look. "What's the matter, Chris?"

He shook his head slightly, then stuck the contraband food under his blanket and reached for Emily's hand.

Emily was so startled, her mouth fell open. As much as she'd yearned for it over the years, Chris had never once made a move on her. She had resigned herself to the fact that, as far as he was concerned, she was only a friend. And sometimes, she feared, not even that.

Now here he was not only holding her hand; he was squeezing it tenderly. "You're so good to me, Emily. I don't deserve it."

Emily was dying, but she summoned the composure to smile, silently thanking her parents and her orthodontist for her now straight, pearly-white teeth. "You deserve... whatever you want, Chris."

Chris peered closely into her flushed face and smiled. "I think I'm in love, Em."

She added a thanks to the Weight Watchers center for helping her slim down from a size twelve to a size nine. "In love?"

"Oh, I know I've had a lot of girlfriends," Chris said with a sheepish smile that had always driven Emily to distraction. "And I'll admit I told most of them I loved them. And maybe at the time—at least with a few—I meant it. This time it's the real thing. I know it's the real thing because I'm so damn miserable." Now he was gripping her hand in earnest, pulling her toward him.

Okay, so she'd imagined far more romantic spots for their first passionate embrace, but she certainly wasn't about to quibble about location.

She fell on him, draping her arms around his neck, only to have her elbow squish right into that double Quarter Pounder stowed away under his blanket.

Chris let out a surprised yelp as a pickle flew out from inside the bun and landed on his neck. An instant later, a pretty brunette in a tight white nurse's uniform swept into the room. Emily sprang off the bed, accidentally pulling some of Chris's blanket with her.

The nurse wagged a finger at Chris as she spied the contraband on the sheet. Then, without a word, she scooped up the mess and deposited it all in a wastebasket, which she removed from the room.

Chris sighed, his gaze fixed on the closed door. "That's her, Em. She's the one. I'm hopelessly in love with her. And the thing that's driving me crazy is, she won't even give me the time of day."

Emily sighed, too. *Tell me about it.*

David at Twenty-Five

"A FASHION photographer?" Alan Freese, David's old roommate from Stanford, gave him an incredulous look. "What about all those dreams you had about becoming a hotshot photojournalist for *Time* or *Newsweek?*"

"This is the nineties, Alan," Liza said dryly. "It's no longer just a woman's prerogative to change her mind." She reached across the table in the small upscale San Francisco café and squeezed David's hand. "And David's definitely a man of the nineties. He's sensitive, open, honest, tender. All the qualities . . ."

Even after all these years David half hoped that she'd finish that sentence with something like, "a woman like me could ever ask for."

"Necessary to make it in the fashion business," was how Liza finished the sentence. "Being in the business myself, I should know. Designing and photographing clothes both take tremendous sensibility, subtlety, awareness. We both have to dig deep into our souls and bare them constantly. We are the work. The work is us."

David smiled at her with a hint of amused affection. "That just about says it all."

Alan rolled his eyes.

Liza slapped Alan playfully on the shoulder. "You know your problem?"

Alan winked at David, then grinned at Liza. "I bet you're going to tell me."

Liza gave Alan a long, contemplative look. "You're still desperately clinging to your outmoded macho eighties image. You have to project a tough, cocky, 'Nothing ever gets to me' persona. You're closing yourself off from your feelings, Alan. You're too self-centered, too aggressive. You don't know how to reach out and make emotional contact." She leaned a little closer to Alan, who'd been smiling wryly through her whole discourse. "You could learn a lot from David. Especially humility."

Alan grinned crookedly at his old school buddy. "You seem to have it all, fellow," he teased, then threw a possessive arm around Liza, nuzzling her neck. "Come on, lover. We better go or we'll be late for that party."

Liza looked earnestly over at David. "You sure you won't come? You might meet someone."

David shook his head, offering to pick up the tab for their drinks so they could take off. He slowly sipped the rest of his martini as he watched Liza slip her arm around Alan's waist and snuggle up against the ruggedly handsome, blond-haired man as they stepped into the street.

Right, he thought. *I've got it all, all right. All except the girl.*

Emily at Twenty-Seven

"THESE PHOTOS ARE GREAT," Emily said enthusiastically, then smiled up at the fashion designer, a dark-haired beauty with incredible violet eyes. "So are the outfits," she added.

Emily also made a note of the outfit Liza Emory was wearing, a provocatively formfitting emerald leather jumper worn over an even more formfitting black bodysuit. By comparison, Emily, wearing a gray pin-striped business suit, felt more like a Midwest schoolmarm, than an assistant editor of *Chic*, an L.A.-based fashion magazine.

"Getting a cover on *Chic* is just the break I need," Liza said with excitement.

Emily slipped off her glasses and resolved to make an appointment at the hairdresser's this week. "Well, I'm not the one that makes the final decision, but I promise I'll put in a good word for you with the boss."

"You mean Mitchell Keniston?" Liza's violet eyes sparkled. "Oh, he was the one that suggested I bring in some of my stuff. We met at a gallery opening last Saturday." She sighed dramatically. "I think he took pity on me because I confessed that I was finding the road to fame and fortune strewn with more potholes than I'd anticipated."

"It is a tough business to break into, but you're very talented." Emily was reflecting on more than the thirty-one-year-old woman's fashion designs; Liza Emory impressed her as a woman who knew how to use her feminine wiles as successfully as she did her sketching pencils.

"Actually," Liza said with a tremor in her honeyed voice, "I'm in a bit of a fix, apartment-wise. Everything is so expensive. An old friend of mine who moved down here just after me is letting me pitch a tent, so to speak, in his studio, but I'm afraid . . . ?"

"You might overstay your welcome?" Emily guessed.

She guessed wrong. Liza laughed softly. "Just the opposite. I'm afraid David will start getting too used to my being around. He's had a kind of puppy-dog crush on me for years."

Emily felt an immediate kinship with this David. Even after all these years, she was still carrying a torch for Chris who was now the exceedingly popular and celebrated sports anchor of a Los Angeles-affiliate network news-show. She couldn't exactly say that they'd grown closer over the years, but Chris did stop by her place on occasion for some strictly platonic TLC—which Emily continued to offer in abundance. That, and the hope that one of these days, Chris would wake up and realize that what had been missing from his life all these years was her.

"I adore David, of course," Liza was saying airily. "He's so good-hearted, so supportive, so nurturing." She gave a graceful little wave of her hand. "My relationship with David is really beside the point."

Emily had a sneaking suspicion she was getting the real point. "You need a place to live."

Liza smiled. "And Mitch tells me you need a roommate."

At least she didn't beat around the bush, Emily thought. And it was true. She might even pick up a few pointers from this femme fatale.

She smiled back at Liza. "Not anymore."

"HI, LIZA, I'M HOME," Emily mumbled wearily, stumbling in the door following a long editing session at the office a couple of weeks after her new roommate had moved in. She heard sounds in the kitchen off to her right. Kicking off her shoes and gathering them in her hand, she walked in to discover a large black Labrador retriever happily munching cereal on her blue-and-white-checked linoleum floor.

Emily grinned as the dog gave her a brief, disinterested study before he returned to his feast.

"Nice to see you, too, Bosco," she said dryly, gathering up the cereal and tidily scooping it into a bowl for him. "I hope you didn't eat Liza first."

The dog emitted a low growl.

Emily sighed, pouring a little more cereal into the bowl. "I suppose Chris thinks I have nothing better to do with my weekends than baby-sit his dog. And where's the old lord and master off to this time? Another romantic escapade with his gorgeous blond co-anchor? Or is it his new lean and lanky brunette stockbroker? No wait. I know. That luscious congresswoman he's had his eye on all month. Tell me, Bosco, when is that man going to wake up and realize that everything he wants is right here in this apartment?"

His bounty devoured, Bosco glanced up at her with what almost looked to Emily to be a sympathetic expression.

"What are you trying to tell me, you mongrel?"

As if on cue, Bosco strutted across the kitchen, nudging open the swing door and slipping into the living room. As the door started to swing shut again, Emily's hand stopped it cold as she caught a glimpse of the pair entwined in each other's arms on the couch.

As much as Bosco had enjoyed munching on his treats in the kitchen, it was nothing compared to the pleasure Liza and Chris seemed to be having, munching on each other.

Her eyes moist and burning, Emily silently let the door swing shut. Everything Chris Anders wanted seemed to be in her apartment after all. . . .

EMILY'S WHOLE BODY WENT numb. "Your . . . what?"

Liza gently touched Emily's cheek. "My maid of honor."

"I . . . Aren't you . . . rushing things? You and Chris have only known each other . . . a few weeks."

"Three weeks, four days and seventeen hours. We both knew it from the minute we set eyes on each other. Oh, Em, please be happy for us. We're so much in love." Suddenly Liza's expression turned sympathetic. "Don't think I'm completely dense. I think I know how you feel about Chris."

"Don't . . ." Emily begged, even resenting Liza addressing her by the nickname that only Chris used.

"I know—or at least I can imagine—that there's nothing worse than pining over a man who just doesn't feel the way about you that you feel about him. If you think about it, I'm really doing you a favor."

Emily gave Liza a rueful look. Favors like that she could do without.

"So, will you be my maid of honor, Em?"

Emily thought about the fact that Chris had been engaged twice before. And both times he'd gotten cold feet. Didn't things usually come in threes? Praying that they would this time around, Emily reluctantly agreed.

1

"ISN'T SHE JUST THE MOST beautiful bride?" Arlene, a fellow editor from *Chic*, gushed as she stood beside Emily on the sidelines watching the newlyweds dance their first postnuptial dance. "She looks like a fairy-tale princess."

Emily nodded grimly. Liza might well look like she'd stepped out of a fairy tale. Emily, however, felt as if she'd stepped into a nightmare. Her attire for the gala wedding didn't help matters any. She was decked out in a ridiculously baroque bridesmaid's gown, an emerald-green taffeta extravaganza, buoyed by poufs of tulle under which were layers of crinoline. Naturally, it was one of Liza's designs—one that Emily felt ought to have ended up on a cutting-room floor and not on her fragile frame.

And then there was the matter of her fragile mind. Up to the last minute, Emily had clung to the belief that the wedding wouldn't come off. As Chris and Liza stood there in the church, the minister smiling beatifically down on them as they began to say their vows, Emily was forced to face the cold, hard truth. There was very little chance that either one of them was going to ditch the other at the altar at this point.

"WOULD YOU LIKE TO dance?"

Emily shifted her gaze from the dazzling newlyweds on the dance floor to Norman Ellis, a balding, ruddy, thirtysomething ad exec at *Chic* that she'd dated a couple of times. To her regret.

She shook her head, mumbling some excuse about her shoes pinching.

"So take your shoes off," he suggested. Norman, as she well knew, was a man who wasn't easily deterred.

"I'll rip my panty hose," Emily muttered.

"Hey, you can take your panty hose off, too."

Emily, who had been trying desperately to stay composed and get through this painful ordeal, suddenly lost it. Glaring contemptuously at Norman, she snapped, "You are a very crass man, Mr. Ellis."

As soon as the words were out, Emily regretted them and mumbled an apology. Not because what she said wasn't true, but because she was venting her anger on the wrong man. It was Chris she wanted to rail at, Chris she wanted to shake. How could he do this to her? How could he be so blind as not to see that Liza would never love him with the intensity, consistency and devotion she had always offered him so willingly? How could he see anything clearly? Chris's vision was seriously blurred by Liza's thousand-watt smile. Not to mention the effect the rest of her physical attributes had on him.

Tears threatened to spill from Emily's eyes as she made a beeline for the reception hall's nearest exit. What was the point, anyway, of standing around at the edge of the dance floor waiting for Chris to ask her to dance? A dance would mean nothing now. Having Chris hold her in his arms at this point would only add to her pain and loss. All those years… Wasted.

Finding a secluded settee hidden behind an ornate pillar in the lobby of the hotel, Emily settled down to have a nice, private, self-pitying cry. She had barely gotten into it, when she heard an odd sound. Like someone else crying. Or, more accurately, trying not to.

Dabbing at her eyes with a linen handkerchief, Emily rose and peeked around the pillar to see a man sitting on a matching settee, sniffing back tears. She recognized the tall, lanky, dark-haired stranger as the fellow who'd given Liza away.

Emily saw a look of profound embarrassment sweep across the man's face the instant he realized he was being observed. He hastily turned away.

Emily smiled sympathetically. "The bride?"

David slowly turned back to look up at her. His reddened eyes narrowed as he observed her more closely. "The groom?"

Emily nodded, a few tears running down her cheeks.

David sighed. Then sniffed.

"Mind if I sit down?"

"Not at all," he said quickly, feeling an instantaneous link with this woman, who, like him, was clearly a member of the unrequited lovers' club.

"Emily Bauer. Briefly, Liza's roommate."

"David Turner. Liza's longtime . . . friend."

They shook hands. Then Emily rummaged in her emerald-green satin clutch for a tissue, which she handed him. While he discreetly blew his nose, she dabbed away at her eyes with her damp hankie and gave him a closer study.

So this was the "David" that Liza had been staying with before moving in with her—the one she'd cavalierly mentioned had had a puppy-dog crush on her for years. Emily thought he was nice looking in a quiet, understated Jimmy Stewart sort of way. Not devastating à la Chris Anders, but perfectly respectable, and most likely trustworthy, steady, sincere. What was wrong with Liza? Couldn't she have appreciated that David Turner was a perfectly good catch? Why did she have to go hooking her bait in someone else's little pond? It was obvious to Emily that David was wildly in love with Liza, while Emily persisted in the belief that Chris was merely infatuated with her—albeit an intense infatuation.

David crumpled the tissue and stuck it in the pocket of his dinner jacket. "Sorry. I don't usually..."

"Neither do I," Emily hastened to say, blinking back a new onslaught of tears.

There was an awkward silence.

"It's a ... nice wedding," he muttered.

"Yes. Nice."

David glanced over at her.

"Have you ... known him long?"

Emily tried to unpouf some of the tulle of her gown—to no avail. "Since second grade. You and Liza?"

David plucked some lint from his black tuxedo trousers. "Third grade."

"A long time," Emily mused.

"Yes. A long time," David concurred.

A protracted silence followed. They looked over at each other at the same time, embarrassed at first, yet feeling an odd kinship.

"I knew it would hurt," Emily blurted out. "But I didn't know how much."

David smiled sympathetically. "You'd think I would have had enough practice dealing with the pain, but ... this time it's so ... final."

Emily handed him another tissue and took one for herself.

"It isn't the kind of wedding I would have had," Emily said softly. "So elaborate and formal. So many people. Even the paparazzi."

"My fantasy was that Liza and I would get married in some picturesque island in Hawaii," David admitted. "In a lush garden overflowing with tropical flowers, Liza with a crown of orchids in her hair, wearing a simple, flowing white dress. Just the two of us and a couple of witnesses. And the minister, of course."

"I dreamed of getting married down in Big Sur. On a windblown cliff overlooking the ocean. Chris and I would each read something from Elizabeth Barrett Browning and there'd be a violinist. Down in the cove a sailboat would be docked. After the wedding Chris and I would sail around for weeks, just the two of us."

"Is he much of a sailor?"

Emily shrugged. "No. Not really."

David sighed. "Come to think of it, Liza may be allergic to orchids. I brought her an orchid corsage for our high-school prom, and she broke out in a rash."

"You went to the prom together?" There was a hint of envy in Emily's voice. "I dreamed Chris would ask me to a prom. He never did. And I never had the courage to ask him to any of mine."

"Well . . . Liza only went with me because her boyfriend broke his leg in a soccer game the day of the prom," David conceded. "I wasn't discouraged. I had it all planned to drive her up to Lookout Point afterward and finally make my move. And then her boyfriend goes and shows up, his leg in a cast, hobbling on crutches."

"Chris broke his leg once. I thought it was going to be the start of something . . . more serious between us."

"I ended up driving Liza up to Lookout Point, all right. Only we weren't alone. While Liza and her soccer star made out in the back seat, I kicked pebbles around outside. In the rain. Feeling like a complete jerk."

"I made the mistake of thinking that Chris was making a pass at me and I practically threw myself at him. Not practically. I did. Only it wasn't me he wanted. There was this nurse. . . . I felt like a total idiot."

They looked at each other and smiled in mutual commiseration. Then David leaned back against the settee, folding his arms across his chest. "I still can't believe it."

Emily scowled. "Neither can I."

"Liza does have a very impulsive nature," David mused. "I've always envied that about her. I'm just the opposite. Plodding, cautious, having to weigh everything from every angle...."

"I'm more compulsive than impulsive. I'm disgustingly organized. I have files for everything. I'm a nut for order and tidiness."

David smiled. "You must have gone crazy, living with Liza. She's not exactly the neatest person."

Emily laughed. "You're being kind." Her expression turned serious. "My guess is, you are kind."

David flushed. "You seem ... kind, too, Emily."

She gave him a wry smile. "Not always. If you want to know the truth, David, I've been having some less-than-kindly thoughts lately. I've found myself wishing that all sorts of terrible things would happen that would prevent this dumb wedding from coming off."

"Me, too."

"I don't even feel guilty," she said defiantly.

"You don't?"

Her self-assertion wavered. "Do you?"

David hesitated. "No. Not ... really."

Emily gave him a sharp look. "Yes, you do."

"Okay," he relented. "A little guilty."

Emily grinned. "Me, too."

"I knew that."

They glanced at each other. Then, unnerved by the intimacy that had somehow gotten established between them so quickly, they both looked away.

"I think I'd better go back in. I promised Liza a dance."

"What?"

"Liza. A dance." He made a twirling motion with his finger.

"Oh. Right. Naturally."

David hesitated. "You can't tell, can you?" he asked finally.

Emily smiled softly, cupping his chin as she carefully inspected his face, thinking again that it was a nice face. "She won't notice a thing." Knowing Liza's tendency to self-absorption, Emily felt sure of that.

He started to rise.

"What about me?" she asked nervously.

He sat back down and gave her face a thoughtful appraisal, finding himself not only evaluating whether she looked like she'd been crying, but assessing Emily's appearance in general. He noted that she had regular, pleasant features, unremarkable in and of themselves, but in combination they made a very attractive package. He particularly liked her mouth. Not full and pouty like Liza's, Emily's mouth formed a sort of ironic slash across her face. Her mouth had personality. He focused on her eyes—warm, brown eyes except that they did look a bit bloodshot. Should he tell her? Or was Emily, like most women he knew—certainly Liza—interested mainly in being told what she wanted to hear?

"Your eyes are a little red."

Emily's brow crinkled. "I knew it."

"Don't worry. The lights are dim in the reception hall."

"What about my nose?"

David thought she had a perfectly fine nose. Even the faint bump in the bridge didn't detract from it.

"Is it shiny?" she asked anxiously.

"Shiny?" He leaned a little closer. "No. Not shiny."

"I forgot to bring along face powder. Or even lipstick. I wasn't thinking too straight this morning when I was getting ready."

David gave her a conspiratorial smile. "I forgot my wallet."

Emily patted his hand, which was resting on his thigh. He, in turn, patted hers. Then they both speedily withdrew their hands.

David sprang up from the settee. "Shall we?"

Emily suddenly felt exposed. "Shall we . . . what?"

David smiled awkwardly. "Go back inside."

EMILY PASTED A BIG SMILE on her face as she reentered the reception hall. David gave her shoulder a little squeeze as he stepped around her and set off in search of Liza.

Strategically placing herself within clear view of Chris, she watched him twirling his beautiful co-anchor around the dance floor. As his eye briefly caught hers, she gave a little wave. He smiled his lady-killer smile.

Twenty-seven years old, and yet she felt like a lovesick adolescent whenever he smiled at her. She smiled dopily back. When the song ended, she hurried over to his side.

"How about one dance with an old friend?" She hoped Chris didn't pick up the nervousness in her voice.

"Well . . . I did promise my bride the next dance." He looked around. When he saw Liza being led onto the dance floor by David, he shrugged and smiled down at Emily.

"So, what do you think, Em?" he asked as he slipped an arm around her waist and began swaying with her to the music.

Emily found it hard to think when she was in Chris's arms, breathing in his intoxicating musky scent, feeling his strong, rugged body against hers. "About . . . what?"

"About what? About my being married?"

If only she could tell him what she really thought about it. Hopeless. Doomed. Heartache just around the corner. Chris and Liza might *look* great together, but Emily believed they were too much alike—both ambitious, competitive, impulsive, each of them used to taking center stage. It was never going to work. Or was that just wishful thinking?

"I think it's great," she lied into his broad chest.

"She's terrific, isn't she? So beautiful and talented. I tell you, Em, I've been dreaming about someone like Liza all my life."

"Isn't it nice that your dream came true?" She could barely get the sentence out and was glad the music was blasting.

"Everything's so perfect. My career, now my personal life. This is so great."

"Great," she echoed mordantly, catching sight of David and Liza a few yards from them on the dance floor. Liza was prattling away, no doubt chewing her lovesick partner's ear off, extolling Chris's virtues. Poor David. Poor her.

Just then David's gaze fell on her. They shared wistful smiles across the dance floor, two suffering souls united in their misery.

EMILY DIDN'T EXACTLY catch the bride's bouquet. It sort of fell uninvited into her hands. Everyone cheered. Norman Ellis came over and put his arm around her. Liza blew her a big kiss. Chris gave her a thumbs-up sign and a wink. From across the room, David gave her a sympathetic shake of the head. Emily shrugged. She was a little tipsy. She wasn't much of a drinker, but she figured if she had to drown her sorrows in something, it might as well be fine French champagne.

The problem was, the champagne hadn't had the desired effect. She felt dizzy, a little queasy, but as miserable as she'd felt when she was stone-cold sober.

While the bride and groom were up in their suite changing for their honeymoon trip to Tahoe, Emily sat alone at a corner table, the bridal bouquet wilting on her lap, trying to decide whether she was going to be truly sick. A hand fell on her shoulder.

At first she thought it was Norman Ellis again, and she was drunk enough to contemplate taking a swing at him.

"Are you okay?"

It wasn't Norman. It was David. She was glad she hadn't swung.

"I'm fine," she lied, producing a brave smile.

"Liar." He slid into a seat beside her. The truth was, he wasn't all too steady on his feet, thanks to imbibing his own fair share of bubbly. It hadn't helped him any more than it had Emily.

She eyed him dryly. "You know me so well."

He smiled crookedly. "I do, Wendy."

"Emily."

"Where?"

"No. I'm Emily. You called me Wendy."

"Did I?"

She leaned a little closer to him. "Have you had too much to drink?"

"No. Absolutely not." He frowned. "Yes."

"Mmm," she said. "I thought so."

He grinned. "So did I."

Emily giggled.

David's grin blinked out. "What's so funny?" Being laughed at, on top of everything else, was more than he could take.

"This bouquet." She held it up over her head, her expression at once sober. As they both studied the floral arrangement, a pert young waitress came along carrying a half-empty tray. Emily's eyes met David's. He nodded. Emily dumped the bouquet unceremoniously on her tray.

"Hey, thanks," the waitress said, brightening.

Emily imitated one of Chris's signature waves. "Don't mention it."

"There, do you feel better now?" David asked her when the waitress had left.

"Yes." She pursed her lips. "No. Not really."

"Would you like to dance?"

"Yes." She rubbed at a gravy stain on one of her poufs. "No. Not really."

"Would you like me to take you home?"

"Yes."

David waited for the retraction. It didn't come.

DAVID STOOD IN THE middle of the living room. "I could smell her perfume the minute I walked in."

"It's Obsession."

He cast her a worried look. "Do you think so?"

"No. I mean her perfume. It's called Obsession. It's all she wears."

"When we were kids she always wore White Shoulders. I used to buy her a bottle of it every year for Christmas. Then, when we were in high school, I found out she'd given her last three bottles to her friend, Buffy."

"That wasn't very nice."

"Oh, Liza didn't have the heart to hurt my feelings. Buffy was happy, anyway. She probably still wears White Shoulders."

He ran his palm along the back of the flower-print couch, eyeing the open door to Liza's ex-bedroom.

"Hers?" he asked hoarsely.

"Mmm."

"Could I . . . ? Would it be okay . . . ?"

"Sure" she said magnanimously. "Go ahead. She's got a ton of stuff in there, but I'm sure she wouldn't mind."

David started across the room, stopping at Liza's open bedroom door.

Emily came up behind him. "The room's pretty messy. Then, that's no surprise to you, right?"

David nodded, casting his eyes wistfully around the room.

"Chris is very tidy," Emily said. "He does make allowances for Bosco, so most likely he will for Liza, too."

"Bosco?"

"His dog."

"Liza isn't wild about dogs."

"I know. I should have said he *did* make allowances for Bosco. He gave the dog to his cameraman."

"I used to have a dog," David said. "Duke. He was run over by a moving van when I was fourteen. I cried for days. I really loved that dog."

"I like dogs. Even Bosco."

He stepped tentatively into Liza's room, carefully maneuvering around a crumpled white silk slip on the floor. "Why didn't Chris give you the dog?"

Emily bent down and picked up the slip. "Oh, he would have, but I guess he thought Bosco would be happier with a family. His cameraman has a wife, a couple of kids . . ." Actually, Emily didn't know that for a fact. She didn't even know if the cameraman was married. All she really did know was that Chris was out having a beer with the guy one evening shortly after Liza started spending most of her nights over at his place. When he'd complained about Bosco and Liza not hitting it off, the cameraman, who was crazy about dogs, offered to take Bosco off his hands. Chris hadn't even thought to ask her if she might like to have the dog herself. Sometimes, Emily conceded, Chris could be a little insensitive. But automatically she made excuses for him. He had a lot of pressures, he always felt under the gun at work, he liked to act on things right away, et cetera, et cetera.

David was standing in front of Liza's bureau, lightly fingering her jars of creams and cosmetics. He unscrewed the cover of her moisture cream and took a deep sniff.

Emily smiled when he turned around. He gave her a quizzical look. She tapped the tip of her nose, then pointed at him. David turned back to the mirror over the bureau. There was a white dot of cream on his nose. He wiped it off.

Emily tossed Liza's slip on her vacated bed, cluttered with an assortment of undergarments, a nightgown, a pair of shoes. David was now at the foot of the bed, his hands gripping the teak frame.

His eyes watered. "I can picture her here, tossing stuff around, frantic over not being able to find a shoe or an earring. She was always misplacing things. One time we spent a whole day searching her room for a missing gold-and-diamond pin. Some guy she was dating had given it to her. It must have cost him an arm and a leg."

Emily sat down on the edge of the bed. "Chris always got fabulous gifts from the women he dated. Rings, cufflinks, cashmere sweaters. One woman even gave him a trophy."

"A trophy?"

Emily nodded.

David's brow crinkled. "A trophy for . . ."

Emily nodded again.

"Oh. Hmm. A trophy." Just what he needed to hear.

He came around the bed and lifted up the slip Emily had tossed on the bedspread. He held it out in front of him, imagining what it would look like with Liza filling it.

Emily gazed up at him, saw the anguished expression on his face. One thing about the guy, he didn't hide his feelings like most men she knew—especially Chris, whom she would best describe as enigmatic. David, by contrast, wore his emotions right on his face like a big neon sign.

"Don't torture yourself like this," she said earnestly. "It doesn't help. Believe me, I know."

He sat down beside her on the bed. "I love her. I've always loved her. I always believed we would end up together. You know, like it was fate."

She put a hand on his shoulder. "I know. I know. The fickle finger of fate."

He put an arm around her waist, noting for the first time that she was slender and shapely. "We're in the same boat."

She gave him a sympathetic hug, discovering that he felt a lot more muscular than his appearance suggested. "We'll survive as long as we keep paddling."

"You're right. You're right," he said, rubbing the small of her back with his palm in a strictly comradely gesture. At the same time, in the tangle of his thoughts and emotions, he found his eyes straying to the strapless bodice of her gown, which accentuated the fullness of her breasts. He might almost call them voluptuous.

"It's just going to take some time." She gave his thigh a reassuring pat, discovering that she liked the hard, firm feel of his flesh. The realization disconcerted her, as if she couldn't quite reconcile her sorrow at having lost Chris with these sensations about the stranger sitting beside her on Liza's bed.

"It does feel like they pulled the rug right out from under us, doesn't it?" His hand moved slowly up her spine. She leaned toward him. He caught the flowery scent of her. Suddenly he felt a bit light-headed, but in a most pleasant kind of way.

"Oh, yes. Yes. Exactly." Her hand lingered on his thigh. Woozily, she worried that he might misconstrue her touch, take it to be suggestive. Then, perversely, she found herself worrying that he wouldn't.

"I can't get the picture of Liza in her wedding gown out of my mind. She made such a beautiful bride. The only problem was . . . I wasn't the groom." His words slurred a bit, his hand falling over Emily's hand, which was still resting on his thigh. Even as he was bemoaning the loss of Liza, he was experiencing this peculiar feeling of sensual anticipation.

"Chris looked glorious. He was made to wear a torpedo . . . I mean, tuxedo. Some men just . . . are." Somehow, as she, too, was slurring her words, her other hand found its way to the collar of David's shirt. Her fingers were toying with his bow tie. A light tug and it came undone. Her hand brushed across his chest. What was she doing? Seducing him? The idea was ludicrous. It was just that bow ties really were so silly.

"You're right. We shouldn't torture ourselves like this." He gave her a peck on the cheek, wondering if what he really had in mind was only simple comfort.

"I know I'm right. I'm so right." She went to "peck" him back, figuring one peck deserved another—only his head shifted and her lips landed smack-dab on his lips. Very nice lips, they were. Warm, soft, slightly parted. Her lips stayed put for a few moments. When she broke away, she felt dizzy and let her head fall back against Liza's pillow.

David swayed a little, his eyes no longer focusing very clearly.

Instinctively, Emily patted the pillow next to her. David kicked off his shoes and stretched out beside her. She began to hum quietly.

"Did you and Chris have a favorite song?" he asked, turning on his side to face her, thinking she had a very appealing profile.

"Not . . . exactly. I always get weepy and think of Chris whenever I hear Frank Sinatra sing . . . 'All the Way.'"

"That's a great song. A great song."

"What about you . . . and Liza?"

"'You Were Meant for Me.'"

She rolled onto her side to face him. "'You Were Meant for Me'?"

"Liza didn't know. About the song. We didn't . . . really have a song. We never really . . ."

"You didn't . . . ?"

Slowly he shook his head, thinking that he ought to be feeling miserable, but somehow he wasn't. Somehow, all he felt like doing was finding out if this sweet, lovely woman's breasts were as voluptuous as he imagined. What would she do if . . . ?

"We didn't . . . either. Chris and I." She found herself edging closer to David. Or was it he who was edging closer to her? She wasn't sure, but she wasn't sorry, either. Her breathing had grown shallow. "Not that I didn't want to. I did. I . . . do."

He looked into her warm brown eyes, feeling a sharp twist of desire. There was something deeply sensual about her eyes. There was something deeply sensual about every single aspect of her.

Emily felt her skin heating up. "I need . . . I think I need to . . . get out of this dumb gown," she blurted out.

"Can I . . . help you?" David offered gallantly.

"That would be . . . very kind of you."

David smiled crookedly. "I'm a very kind man."

No sooner had he unzipped her gown, than Emily gave him what began as a warm appreciative kiss, but quickly turned into something urgent and greedy. David's hands cupped her bare breasts—soft, firm, and even more voluptuous than he'd imagined. Within minutes they were both naked and fiercely embracing each other, neither of them quite as tipsy as they told themselves they were, both of them in the grip of a powerful hunger to which their bodies surrendered, frenzied and frantic.

"This doesn't make . . . any sense," she murmured at some point, their bare limbs entwined around each other.

His hand moved down her flat belly. "Does anything . . . make sense?" David answered huskily, his warm breath whispering against the side of her face.

"No. No . . . it doesn't," she agreed.

His hand moved lower still, slipping a little inside her, up and down with feathery strokes. And suddenly she was saying—no, crying out with abandon—"Yes. Oh, yes!"

As he swung his body over her, Emily temporarily came to her senses. "Wait. You need . . ."

"Oh, no. I didn't bring . . . I never thought . . ."

"Wait. Wait." She jackknifed up to a sitting position and pulled open the top drawer of Liza's bedside table with so much force it almost fell right into her lap. After a couple of frantic moments of rummaging through it, she came up with just what she suspected she'd find—a handful of tinfoil packets.

A few moments later David slipped easily inside her, filling her. Emily sighed a long, pleasurable sigh. He began to move, his rhythm jerky and awkward at first, but then smoothing out, like a skater who hasn't been on the ice for a while and needed a little practice.

Emily hadn't been "on the ice" for a while herself, but after a few moments of fumbling, her rhythm came back, too.

At first, Emily was aware of the harsh sound of their mingled breathing. Then he kissed her—a deep, desperate kiss— and she stopped paying attention to sounds. For the first time in weeks, life began to take on shape and color for her and she abandoned herself to wave after wave of pleasure.

"I want you. Please. Yes, yes," Emily cried, closing her eyes, unable to stop herself from imagining it was Chris who was making love to her with such ardor. A dream come true. . . .

"I need you. I need this . . . so much," David gasped, the fantasy taking hold of its own volition that this was Liza beneath him, Liza moaning her pleasure, Liza wanting him. Him. Only him. Fate . . .

And then they stopped talking, even stopped fantasizing, both of them submerged in the rhythm of it, the joy, the exhilaration, the pure blur of intoxicating sensation.

2

THEY WOKE UP AT THE crack of dawn. In bed together. In Liza's bed, no less. Neither of them moved or even risked opening their eyes. Opening their eyes meant facing each other. Worse, it meant confronting what they had done.

We were drunk, Emily told herself. *We didn't know what we were doing. I certainly didn't, anyway.* Even as she was denying responsibility for her actions, she knew she was lying. She had wanted him. At least, she had wanted someone. Who was she kidding? She had wanted Chris. Just as she was certain David had wanted Liza. David. Except for his name and the fact that he was madly in love with her ex-roommate, she didn't even know him. She'd gone to bed with a total stranger. What must he think of her? Forget what he thought of her; she thought poorly enough of herself.

How could she forget him, though? He was lying right there beside her. Separated by a matter of inches. Stark-naked, just like her.

She squeezed her eyes shut, hoping he would just slip off without a word. After all, what could he possibly say to her? What could she say to him? That they were both lonely, hurting, needy, and so they'd settled for what was available? It sounded so heartless, so cheap, so cold. She wasn't like that at all. She guessed that David wasn't, either.

He stirred. She froze.

"Emily?" he whispered tentatively.

When she made no response, David found himself wondering if maybe it wouldn't be easier for them both if he just ducked out without a word. He couldn't believe what had happened between them. Not that Emily wasn't a perfectly nice, attractive woman. A perfectly desirable woman. She also happened to be a perfect stranger. And he was in love with another woman. He'd taken advantage of Emily. He knew she'd had too much to drink. He knew she'd been feeling particularly vulnerable. He'd made the first move into Liza's bedroom. . . .

How many years had he dreamed of one day being in Liza's bed? The irony of it, to finally be here . . . with another woman.

He glanced around the room as if searching for fire exits.

"Good . . . morning," she said finally, unable to bear the silence and discomfort any longer.

"How are you?" His tone had the solicitous ring of a doctor paying a house call on an ailing patient. Only in this case it was the doctor who was ailing.

How could Emily tell him the truth? How could she tell him that she felt sick with shame, disgusted with herself for having been so promiscuous? She might not know David very well, but she sensed that he was sensitive, vulnerable, unsure enough of himself as it was. She couldn't blame him for what happened last night. Not when she'd participated so enthusiastically.

"I'm fine. Just . . . fine," Emily replied politely.

David turned to face her, meeting her profile. "You look very nice in the morning." He meant that. Emily might lack that dazzling cover girl beauty of Liza, but she was very pretty in her own quiet way. He particularly liked how her auburn hair fell in soft waves about her face. And he remembered more than liking the way her voluptuous silken body had felt over him last night.

She allowed herself a quick glance at him. "Thank you. So do you." She knew he thought she was just saying that to be polite, which in part she was, but she meant it, too. Okay, David lacked the dashing, rugged allure of Chris, but he was a perfectly attractive man. Dressed, he had a thin, almost skinny appearance, but undressed she'd been able to see that he was neatly muscled and lean in a graceful, sinewy way.

Not that it mattered. She was certainly never going to see him again. It would be too awkward. She was sure he felt the same way, even though he was trying to be very decent about the whole thing. She was doing her best, as well.

David lay there thinking about his formal attire lying crumpled on the floor. How was he going to discreetly get out of bed and get dressed? He glanced at his watch. "Will you look at that? It's almost seven."

"That late?" She wasn't about to tell him that most Sunday mornings she slept till noon. Then again, most Sunday mornings she slept alone. In her own bed.

She rolled over slightly to see whether she could spot some item of apparel close to the bed that she could throw on. Some of the blanket rolled with her, leaving David unexpectedly and alarmingly exposed.

"Oh, I'm . . . sorry," Emily said, her cheeks burning. She quickly returned to her prior position, flat on her back, her eyes cast up to the ceiling.

David shot her a look. "About last night, Emily. . ."

"Oh, please, David. You don't have to say . . ."

"I just want to say you were . . . great."

"Thank you very much." He might have been praising a term paper she'd written. *Thank you, Professor. I'm so glad you liked my grammar, style and punctuation.*

"I had a very nice time," she said, her voice strained. "That is . . . I thought you were . . . great, too." Which, separate from the embarrassing circumstances, was the truth. Their love-making had been surprisingly torrid and sensual. Her cheeks reddened as she recalled the exultant cry she'd uttered when she'd reached orgasm.

He smiled crookedly. "You didn't have to say that. Just because I said . . ."

"Oh, but I wanted to."

Their eyes met for a brief moment of candor. Emily thought, *He looks so vulnerable*. David thought, *She looks so unprotected*. Both filled with regret and embarrassment, they looked away at the same time.

"Would you like . . . a shower?" she asked after an extended silence.

David's brow creased. Shower? Yes, he wanted a shower. Not here, however. Not in the shower that Emily used. Not to mention Liza. The image of Liza and Chris entwined in each other's arms flashed in his mind. Almost as soon as the image sharpened, it altered. Suddenly he was seeing himself and Emily au naturel. . . .

"Why don't you go and shower first?"

Emily nodded. "Okay." Still, she made no move.

It took a few moments for it to dawn on him that she might feel uncomfortable about jumping out of bed naked.

"I'll just close my eyes and . . . go back to sleep for a few minutes," he mumbled, pulling the covers up over his face.

He couldn't see it, but Emily smiled appreciatively as she made a beeline for the door.

EMILY WAS DRESSED IN a pair of old jeans and a worn Forty-Niners sweatshirt, and had coffee brewing when David stepped out of Liza's bedroom. It was amusing to see him all dressed up in his tux, the outfit looking a little the worse for wear. As did David himself. There were dark spots under his eyes and he was holding his head at a funny angle. A hangover, she surmised. Her own head wasn't exactly in A-1 condition either. She vowed never to drink champagne again.

"Smells good," David said, trying to sound upbeat. Truthfully the smell of coffee was making his stomach lurch. "You shouldn't have . . . gone to so much trouble." That was an understatement.

The toast popped up. Emily grabbed it too soon, burning her fingertips. She hadn't wanted to make David breakfast, meager as it was, but it seemed so callous to toss him out without any of the requisite niceties that she felt should follow a night of passion—however much remorse she might be feeling the morning after.

"Here you are," she said, averting her eyes as she set two servings of dry toast on two plates across from each other at the kitchen table. "Oh, do you want butter?" She darted to the fridge, examining its contents as if her life depended on it. "Jam? Strawberry? Blackberry? Raspberry? Or cheese? I think we have some cheese. . . . Swiss? Cheddar? No, forget the Cheddar. It looks a little moldy."

"Some butter would be fine."

She pulled a butter dish out of its special compartment. "I only have margarine." When she looked over at him, her expression had achieved some composure.

"Margarine is fine. Better for your heart."

"Right. And cheaper."

"True."

"I'm so used to it, butter tastes funny." She sat down. David followed suit across from her.

"I know what you mean."

"Oh, the coffee. I forgot all about the coffee." She popped back up, relieved to have something else to attend to, besides joining David in an anything-but-cozy breakfast for two.

"Milk?"

"No. Black is fine."

Emily nodded. "Me, too."

She set a steaming mug in front of him, then went back to pour a second mug for herself.

"Good coffee," David said politely.

"You don't think it's too strong?" She'd been so distracted when she was getting the coffee ready, she'd lost count of the scoops.

"No," he lied. "I like it strong."

He buttered his toast, trying his best not to hurry it. Trying, as he bit into it, not to just gobble it up and wash it down with some of the strongest coffee he'd ever tasted. He didn't want her to guess how eager, how desperate he was to flee.

Emily buttered her toast, wondering how she was going to swallow it. Her stomach was tied in knots. All she wanted was for David to hurry up and leave so that she could get started on forgetting that she'd ever met him.

He brushed some crumbs off his tuxedo jacket. "I feel a little silly being all dressed up like this on a Sunday morning."

"It's still very early. I doubt you'll run into many people on your way home." Wherever home was. Far from her home, she hoped.

"At least I don't have all that far to go."

Batting zero so far, Emily thought, biting into her toast.

David glanced aimlessly around the kitchen, his gaze falling on the wall clock shaped like an apple. "I suppose they're in Tahoe by now." Slowly, he looked over at Emily. Their gazes met and held for the first time that morning.

"It's probably nice there this time of year," she said softly.

David nodded, but then his lips curled up mischievously. "I hope it rains."

Emily grinned. "Pours."

"A hurricane."

They both laughed, but their glee was strictly temporary.

"Well . . ."

"Well . . ." Emily echoed.

"I guess I should be . . . heading home."

"Oh, right. Me, too. I mean . . . I am home, but I have to . . . go off and do some errands." Precisely what errands she was supposed to be doing at eight o'clock on a Sunday morning, she had no idea.

David rose slowly and smiled—a decent, good-natured smile. For an instant, she wished their night of passion had meant something to them both.

"Thanks, Emily. For the coffee and toast. For . . . everything."

"Don't mention it," she said, trying to sound bright and cheery but not quite pulling it off.

They walked together to the front door, both of them feeling absurd as they stood there trying to find a way of saying goodbye that wouldn't be utterly awkward.

"I'll be seeing you, Emily."

She stuck out her hand. "Take care of yourself, David."

He took her hand, but instead of giving it a shake, he squeezed it, then leaned over and gave her a short, sweet kiss on the lips.

As soon as he left, Emily fell against the closed door, limp, drained, shaken. She pressed her eyes shut. "This is all your fault, Chris Anders," she said aloud to the empty room.

DAVID STEPPED INTO HIS apartment, a spacious and attractive loft with windows that ran from floor to ceiling at the north end, the ceiling being two stories high. Light poured in and warmed the space. He headed straight past his studio to the living area, which was cordoned off by decorative half-walls and ornately carved alabaster pillars. The entire loft oozed architectural detail, all provided by the last tenant, an interior designer from whom David had sublet the place for a year.

Liza had been the one to talk him into taking the loft, despite the fact it was a little "lofty" for both his taste and his budget. So, why had he let her talk him into it? The answer was easy. He'd hoped that she would love it—if not him— enough to stay there with him permanently.

Instead, she'd moved in with Emily. And the rest—as they say—was history.

His phone rang. For half a second, he was afraid it was Emily. That was ridiculous. He was sure she wanted no more to do with him than he did with her.

"Hello."

It was Alan Freese, his old college buddy and Liza's former lover, on the other end of the line. "David. Thank God. I've been ringing you half the night and all morning. I was ready to call the police, worried you might have gone and done something really dumb after Liza's wedding."

"I did," David muttered.

"What?"

"No . . . nothing. Forget it. I'm fine. How about you?"

"Come on, Davey, I got Liza out of my system years ago. Although I do admit I felt a little miffed when she didn't invite me to her wedding. Besides, I would have liked to be there if, for nothing else, to give you some moral support." There was a brief pause. "So, are you going to tell me where you were all night?"

"No."

"Are you sure you're okay? You sound strange."

"Maybe that's because the laugh's on me."

"Don't be so hard on yourself. I wouldn't say this if we were face-to-face because you'd probably sock me in the jaw, but . . . she isn't worth it, David. No woman is, if you ask me."

"I didn't ask you."

"Okay, okay. I know you've been nuts about her practically your whole life, but...in a way...I know her better than you."

"What are you trying to do? Rub salt into the wound?"

"You know me better than that," Alan said, clearly hurt. "I wish to hell you had slept with her, had an affair with her. Then maybe you could have gotten her out of your system like I did."

"Well," David said wistfully, "We'll never know at this point if that's what would have happened, will we?"

"There are plenty of other fish in the sea, Davey."

"Gee," David said dryly, "did you just make that up?"

"All I'm trying to say is . . . Oh, forget it. If you want to spend the rest of your life hung up on her, that's your business."

"I don't intend to spend the rest of my life hung up on anyone," David said resolutely. Then Emily Bauer suddenly popped into his mind. She was not a welcome visitor. He'd probably feel guilty and embarrassed for the rest of his life over his one-night stand with Emily. Would he feel any better if it was more than a one-night stand? He gave his head a sharp shake as if to dislodge such a crazy notion. What was he thinking? He certainly wasn't capable of thinking straight at the moment. But who could blame him?

"Are we still on for squash this afternoon?"

"What?"

"Squash? A game with a small, hard ball that you whack against a wall. . . ."

"Funny guy."

"So? Two-thirty like usual?"

David hesitated. "I don't really feel up to it. How about a rain check?"

"You sure? I hate to think about you sitting around that studio of yours, moping all day."

"I don't plan to mope. I plan to work. I've got a pile of touch-ups to do."

"Yeah, sure. I understand. Look, give me a buzz if you change your mind later, or if you just want to chew the fat, or go get plastered...."

"Thanks, Alan, but I think I'll go on the wagon for a while. I'll be in touch soon. And... thanks for calling."

After he hung up, David fell across his bed, snatching up a silver-framed photo of Liza from off his bedside table. He hugged it to him, but was immediately assaulted with memories of hugging Emily to him last night. How could he ever face her if they ran into each other again? He would just have to do his best to make sure that didn't happen.

WHEN EMILY'S DOORBELL rang about ten minutes after David left, she froze. Who would come calling at eight-fifteen on a Sunday morning? It had to be David. He must have left something behind. *Okay,* Emily told herself. *Act casual and as if nothing had happened. Ha!*

"Forget something?" she asked with false cheeriness as she flung open the door.

Only it wasn't David standing in her doorway. It was her mother. Naomi Bauer, a tall, slender, well-dressed woman with expertly frosted short blond hair, had moved to L.A. two years ago, right after her divorce from Emily's father who was now living in Sarasota, Florida, with his twenty-six-year-old wife and former dental hygienist. Naomi had come west to be close to her only child—frequently too close for Emily's comfort.

"Forget something?" Naomi Bauer echoed, giving her daughter a curious look. "What would I have forgotten? I just got here."

Emily felt her cheeks redden. "I thought you were... someone else."

"Obviously."

"I thought you were my neighbor, Janis. She's always leaving things behind."

Naomi didn't believe her daughter for one minute, but let it go. As she stepped into the apartment, she handed a heavy shopping bag over to Emily. An aroma of cinnamon and apples wafted from the bag.

"What are you doing here at this hour, Mother?"

"I figured maybe you'd be up early today. To be honest, I figured maybe you didn't sleep so well last night. After all, it's not every day that the man you love gets married. To someone else."

Emily rolled her eyes. "Please, Mother . . ."

"Okay, okay, I'm not going to say another word." She scrutinized her daughter. "You look terrible."

"I feel fine."

"Don't lie to your mother."

Emily had to laugh. Then she peered into the shopping bag. "The pie smells heavenly."

"Your favorite."

Emily smiled. "I know that. Thanks, Mom."

"Don't eat too much of it, though. You don't want to blow up like a blimp."

"Don't worry."

"On the other hand, you do look a little scrawny, Emily. A few pounds wouldn't hurt."

"I'm not scrawny. I'm a perfectly good weight for my size."

After slipping off her jacket, Naomi took the shopping bag back from Emily and marched into the kitchen.

"Mom, I was just about to climb back into bed," Emily said, tagging after her mother.

"How come you're dressed?"

"So what? People are capable of sleeping in their clothes." Why hadn't she thought of that last night?

"How was the wedding?" Naomi asked, as Emily set the shopping bag on the table. Then Naomi noticed the two coffee mugs and two plates scattered with crumbs.

Emily scooped up the dishes and headed for the sink. "The wedding was very nice," she said, her back to her mother. Then she pivoted around to face her. "I don't want to talk about it. Any of it," she said pointedly.

Naomi held out her hands. "What did I say?"

"It isn't what you said. It's what you're thinking."

"So now you're a mind reader?"

Emily's fingers pressed into her temples. "I need some aspirin."

"Better still, some antacid," Naomi countered.

Emily was about to argue—it was mostly out of habit—but she decided the antacid was a better choice for what ailed her. For at least part of what ailed her. There was no known cure that she knew of for the other part.

Her mother, however, had a cure for everything. "Give it time, Emily. Time heals all wounds."

"There should be a law against spouting platitudes at eight-thirty on a Sunday morning," Emily said dryly, plucking out the box of antacid from her kitchen cabinet and fixing herself a glass of the fizzy drink.

"A platitude?" Naomi looked affronted. "Who should know better than me that what I'm saying is the absolute truth. Do I still pine over your father?" Before Emily could answer, she said, "I do not."

"Please, could we change the subject?" Emily pleaded, swallowing down the drink with a little shiver.

"Okay. Okay. Let's have some pie."

Naomi commenced to cut two generous slices of her homemade apple pie and set them on plates. Next, she sampled the coffee, made a face and started over again.

"I can't eat anything now, Mother. I'm just not hungry."

"Why should you be hungry?" Naomi's eyes slid to the sink. "You obviously already had breakfast. Sit down and watch me eat. I'm starving. I couldn't eat a thing last night, worrying about you."

"Why were you worrying about me?"

Naomi shrugged. "No, you don't want to talk about it."

Emily sat down across from her mother, propping her elbows on the table and letting her chin sink into her cupped palms. "Okay, I was pretty miserable watching Chris and Liza . . ." She let the sentence trail. "I don't know how I could have clung to the belief all these years that Chris would suddenly see the light."

"I must say that in the end I didn't believe he'd settle for flash over substance." Naomi sighed. "Maybe all men do in the end. Look at your father."

Yes, Emily thought. And look at David pining away for Liza, who, for Emily's taste, was strictly flash. If only she could have been a "flash in the pan."

Naomi pushed aside her half-eaten plate of pie and leaned closer to her daughter. "So, are you going to tell me who you ate breakfast with this morning?"

Emily gave her mother a level look. "No."

Naomi drew her plate back in front of her and resumed eating, before pausing again.

"Are you planning any more meals with this person?"

Emily sighed with exasperation. "I don't believe you. You never let up. I happen to be a grown woman, Mother. And my personal life is just that. Mine." She brushed a strand of hair away from her eyes. "And no, I'm not planning to have any more meals with this person. I'm not planning to ever see this person again. There, are you happy now?"

Naomi rose and came around the table to her daughter. She cupped Emily's head against her breast. "How can I be happy when you're so unhappy?"

Tears broke from Emily like a dam. Not that she minded sobbing in front of her mother. She'd done it before, over the years. And one thing about Naomi: She'd always been sympathetic to her plight. Even doing her best to offer motherly advice on how she might win her man. Emily knew that it was almost as much of a disappointment for her mother as it was for her that Chris had up and married another woman.

"Emily, Emily. You'll find someone else," Naomi soothed, as her daughter's sobs eventually downshifted into sniffles.

"Not someone like Chris." No sooner were the words out than she thought of David. To say that David wasn't like Chris was an understatement. David wasn't physically imposing. He didn't exude an air of authority and containment. He lacked that roguish charm, that sexy Southern drawl, that wildly flirtatious smile.

So, why was she even thinking about David? She certainly didn't *want* to be thinking about him. She wanted to forget she'd ever met him; forget blindly groping for him, undressing him, stroking him, crying out for him. A wave of alarm crested, broke over her. What if she couldn't get him out of her mind? That was all she needed. Shifting her affections from the man who had married Liza to the man who was in love with her!

Never.

"There," Naomi said softly, smoothing her daughter's hair away from her face. "Better?"

"Much better," Emily said with firm resolve. She wasn't about to subject herself to any in-depth emotional scrutiny. Not now.

3

"SO, WHAT DID YOU THINK of the spread?"

Emily looked across the large mahogany desk at her attractive gray-haired boss, Mitchell Keniston, the heart and soul of *Chic*. "I wish we could have inked out the maid of honor."

Keniston grinned as he glanced down at the open pages of this month's issue featuring the wedding of up-and-coming fashion designer, Liza Emory, and local celebrity sportscaster, Chris Anders. "What are you talking about? You look great in these photos. That gown of yours was wild, probably one of Liza's best designs. Only topped by her wedding gown."

Emily, who thought she looked like an ostrich gone amok in her plumed emerald-green gown, muttered, "I guess it just isn't . . . me."

Mitchell Keniston gave his head a shake. "I don't know why you're always putting yourself down, Emily. You looked dynamite at Liza's wedding. Why, if I weren't twenty years too old and ten years too married, I would definitely have made a play for you myself."

Emily merely smiled. Being twenty years too old and ten years too married hadn't stopped Mitch Keniston from making a play for Liza. Fortunately for Mitch's wife and three sons, Chris's quick appearance on the scene dashed any hopes Mitch might have had for straying from the fold.

"I noticed you didn't do too badly for yourself at the bash. You and that pal of Liza's looked comfy-cozy at that table for two," Mitch said with a smile that Emily took to be sala-cious. Then again, maybe it was just her guilty conscience.

"Oh, he wasn't . . . anyone . . . special," Emily mumbled, averting her eyes. "We just . . . talked. Nice guy and all, but . . ."

"But, nothing," Mitch said, his expression turning abruptly paternalistic. "It's high time you found yourself a nice, solid young man. It isn't any secret around here that you had your heart set on Chris Anders."

Emily jumped up from her chair. "Please, Mitch. Chris and I are lifelong friends. It's never been anything more than that. Whatever silly rumors have been floating around here . . . Well, that's all they are. I must get back to work now."

"Emily."

She was almost at the door. "Yes?"

"You haven't forgotten about filling in for me tonight at the Reimans' cocktail party."

Emily *had* forgotten all about it. A cocktail party was the last place she wanted to be tonight. Ever since the wedding three weeks ago, she'd been in hibernation. Friends from work hadn't even been able to cajole her into going to a movie or getting a pizza after work. And no amount of coaxing from her mother had gotten Emily over to her apartment for din-ner.

Turning down her boss was another story. "The Reimans'. Right."

"Seven-thirty. You've got the address on the Rolodex file. It's over in Palos Verdes. Be sure to shower Beverly Evans with accolades. We want to beat out *Glamour* and *Vogue* for a preview of her spring collection. We've got a bit of an edge because she's based here in L.A., but I'm sure New York is wooing her like crazy."

"I have a feeling she'd much prefer getting those accolades directly from the master wooer, himself," Emily said, hop-ing Mitch would change his mind and go himself.

"I would if I could, but Phyllis is receiving an award to-night from some charity group or other, and I made a sol-emn promise that I'd be there. Believe me, I'd much rather be at the Reimans'."

Emily nodded, thinking that made one of them. Not for the first time in the past three weeks, she thought about leaving *Chic*, leaving L.A. altogether. There was really nothing for her here now. Nothing spelled C-H-R-I-S.

"THIS IS THE FIFTH TIME I've beat you in three weeks. A rec-ord. Liza ought to get married more often," Alan Freese teased good-naturedly as he and David headed off the squash court.

David wiped his sweaty face with a towel, then threw it at his friend. "No one's ever going to accuse you of being one of those New Age sensitive guys."

Alan grinned. "You've just got to start putting things into perspective."

"Spoken like a true lawyer."

"A true divorce lawyer," Alan corrected with a wink.

"You don't think they're going to last either, do you?"

Alan smoothed back his damp sandy-blond hair, then swung an arm around David. "If I say I think it won't last, then I'm helping you keep that torch burning. What you need is a nice big wind to come along and blow the damn thing out." He glanced over at his friend. "What about that hot lit-tle number you spent the night with after the wedding?"

David stopped short, his face red. "How the hell did you know about Emily?"

"Oh, Emily. Nice name."

David shrugged off Alan's arm from his shoulder. "Some-times you can be one big pain in the—" He swallowed the rest of the sentence as two attractive young women passed by.

"So, is Emily the reason you can't go to the hockey game with me tonight?"

"No," David said tightly, hating himself for having fallen right into his friend's trap. "She is not the reason. I am not seeing Emily, tonight or any other night. I have absolutely no interest in seeing her again. I've got to go to some dumb cocktail party tonight over in Palos Verdes."

EMILY'S PHONE WAS ringing as she walked into her apartment that evening after work. It was a little past six-thirty and she had to change into something cocktail-partyish to be at the Reimans' place in the hour. She decided to ignore the phone and let her machine take the message.

She wasn't surprised when she heard her mother's voice after the beep.

"Emily? Emily, are you there? I hate these machines. And I hate it even more when you deliberately don't pick up the phone. I know you don't believe in ESP, but I swear I can always tell when you're there or not. You're there now, I know it."

Emily had to smile.

"So, all I want to know is, how are you taking the news? You did watch the news tonight, didn't you? That is, you watched Chris do sports. Only it was more than sports tonight, wasn't it? Oh, Emily, I hope you're not sitting there sulking. If you ask me—under the circumstances—I think it's for the best."

Emily snatched up the phone. "What's for the best?"

"I knew you were there."

"I just walked in. And I'm in a hurry."

"A date?"

"No, Mother. A business function. Now, what's for the best?"

"You didn't watch Chris tonight?"

Emily scowled. "I told you. I just walked in. Besides, it's not like I rush home every night and switch on my TV so I can get a glimpse of Chris Anders on the boob tube." *Liar.* She did her best not to miss him. If she came home too late to catch him on the six o'clock news, she was sure to be tuned in for his spot at eleven.

"You're so irritable lately, Emily. Are you eating properly? I know when I don't eat well, I get so constipated—"

"Enough, Mother."

There was a brief pause during which Emily heard her mother's low sigh. "I hate to be the one to tell you." Another pause. Another sigh, this one louder and more dramatic. "He's leaving."

Emily's first thought was that Chris was leaving Liza. Then she realized he wasn't likely to announce that kind of news after giving the hockey and basketball scores. "Leaving? You mean leaving the show?"

"Leaving L.A."

Emily blinked furiously, as if caught in a car's high beams. "Leaving L.A.?"

"For New York."

Emily had to grab onto the edge of the table to keep her balance. New York. She'd never see him again. He might as well be dropping off the face of the earth.

"It's a big step up for him, dear. He's going to co-anchor a network prime-time sports show. At least you'll be able to watch him on TV."

Some consolation. "But . . . Liza. All her connections are here."

"Maybe. But, she must be supporting the move. I remember when we were living in Chicago and your father landed that job with the Merrish Company in Stanford, Connecticut, I packed everything up and followed along like a good little wife." There was an edge of bitterness in Naomi's voice.

"Anyway," she went on, "New York and Paris are still the fashion meccas of the world as far as most designers are concerned. Liza might do even better on the East Coast."

"Yes," Emily said weakly. "I suppose it's a good career move for both of them. I'll have to send Chris a . . . a congratulations card."

"You sound so depressed, dear. I know how hard it is to accept that he's married now. Although I firmly believe the two of them—"

"Please, Mother."

Naomi shrugged. "Maybe this move of his is for the best. You know what they say. Out of sight, out of mind."

Emily had to bite her tongue to keep from pointing out that the old cliché hadn't worked very effectively for her mother. Even though her parents had been divorced for two years and lived thousands of miles apart, Emily knew her mother hadn't managed to get Jason Bauer out of her mind; nor did the distance keep her from hoping that one day he would come to his senses. Emily was afraid another old cliché was more apt where she and her mother were concerned. *Absence makes the heart grow fonder.*

"I've got to go, Mother. I'm going to be late for this cocktail party."

"Oh, a cocktail party." Naomi's voice perked up. "Why don't you wear that gorgeous red dress I talked you into buying last month? You look very good in that dress, Emily. The color brings out the pink in your skin tone and is wonderful for your hair. And besides, men adore red."

THE PARTY WAS IN FULL swing when Emily arrived. She slowly wove her way through the crowd, glass of soda water in hand, nodding every few steps to a familiar face, trying to avoid getting drawn into any of the clusters. Emily invariably felt as if she stuck out like a sore thumb at these glamorous gatherings. Even in her sizzling red dress, which she hadn't worn because of her mother's hope that it would rouse some man's interest, but because, after their phone conversation, she'd been too rattled to think about what to wear.

Finding a quiet corner, Emily took a sip of her soda water, then checked her watch, debating how much longer she needed to stay. She had, as promised, done what she'd come here to do—namely, pay tribute to L.A.'s doyenne of fashion designers. She was sure Mitch would have done a much better job of it, but at least she did consider Beverly Evans a fine designer. Otherwise it would have been hard for her to sing the woman's praises. Emily had never been good at deceit.

Glancing aimlessly across the room, she spotted George Silverman heading her way. George was a veteran fashion photographer whom she liked. She started to wave when she saw David Turner—of all people—right behind George. What in heaven's name was he doing here?

Suffused with panic, Emily searched for an escape route. Too late. He'd already seen her. And looked as surprised and upset as she was sure she looked.

DAVID'S GAZE WAS DRAWN to the red dress and the very striking figure filling it. It was only when his eyes trailed slowly up to the woman's face that he blanched. For an instant he told himself he was mistaken. It couldn't be Emily. What would Emily be doing here? Then he remembered Liza telling him, before she moved out of his studio to room with Emily, that her new roommate worked at *Chic* magazine. Somehow it hadn't sunk in. He supposed it was because Emily didn't fit his stereotype of a fashion-magazine editor. And he'd met enough of them over the past few years to form a stereotype.

Okay, so he'd figured out what she was doing here. Now the question was, what was he going to do? She'd spotted him spotting her, so there was no way he could pretend he hadn't spotted her and slip off. Further dashing any prospect of escape, his friend George swung around and took a firm hold of his arm.

"Come on," George said amiably. "There's someone I want you to meet. A gal who hates these shindigs almost as much as you do."

"I don't doubt it," David muttered.

NOT KNOWING WHAT ELSE to do, Emily extended her hand to David as they were introduced, pretending she didn't know him. David, taking her lead, followed suit. Clammy palm met clammy palm.

"David, here, is aces in the business," George said effusively. "You should know, Emily. He did the photos for that first spread you ran in *Chic* of that designer— What's her name again?"

David swallowed. "Liza Emory."

Emily stared at David. Over her years in the business, Emily had formed her own stereotypes of fashion photographers and David Turner didn't fit the stereotype. Not at all. Not that this observation was nearly as disconcerting as realizing that she'd actually slept with a man whose profession she hadn't even known—along with the multitude of other things she didn't know about David Turner.

"You do very good work, David," she said tightly, her gaze already shifting to George even before David uttered a hoarse, "Thanks."

"It's been a while, George," Emily said, trying to put a little life into her voice, but not succeeding all that well. "Those photos you took of Hollywood's new starlets in *Vanity Fair* last month were fabulous."

George grinned. "Yeah, it's a hellish job, but somebody's gotta do it," he said, giving David a little nudge.

David managed a weak laugh. All Emily could manage was a half smile.

"Say, what are you drinking?" George asked her. "Champagne?"

Emily could feel her cheeks heat up, just remembering the trouble she'd gotten herself into the last time she'd drunk champagne. "No. No, just club soda."

"Come on, Emily. Live a little. The champagne at this shindig's top-notch." George plucked her glass from her hand. "Don't move. Either one of you. I'll bring us all back some of the bubbly."

"Oh, none for me," David mumbled.

"I was just about to leave," Emily muttered.

George wagged a finger at her. "You can't leave yet. We just got here."

Emily and David watched George slip through the crowd. They kept on watching long after he'd disappeared, long after it was obvious that they both were at a complete loss for what to say to each other.

Finally, it became more awkward not to talk than to say something. They ended up speaking at the same time.

"You first," David said gallantly.

"Oh . . . Nothing, really. It's a . . . nice party. What was it you said?"

"Pretty much the same thing."

They eyed each other for a moment, then looked away.

What now? David agonized. *Am I supposed to lie and tell her I've been meaning to call? I say that, and then she has to lie and say something like. "Oh, well, I'd love to hear from you sometime. When we're not both incredibly busy."*

"I really hate these 'shindigs,' as George calls them," Emily admitted.

"Me, too," David confessed.

She glanced over at him. "Did you…hear about Chris and Liza? That they're moving to New York?"

David nodded. "Yeah. I spoke to Liza yesterday and she told me."

Emily felt envious that Liza had been considerate enough to tell David directly.

"I'm not really surprised," he went on in a flat tone. "She always wanted to end up in The Big Apple."

"Chris, too. I always knew he'd make it big one day. He's got . . . what it takes."

"Yeah, I suppose he does," David said dryly.

Emily didn't say anything, but she was thinking the same was true about Liza. She felt David's eyes on her, but didn't meet his gaze.

"Are you . . . okay?" he asked softly.

Emily wasn't okay, but she was afraid that if she admitted that to David, he might admit to her that he wasn't okay, either. Which she knew he wasn't. All you had to do was look at him to know that. So, then they might start to commiserate with each other again, and then one thing might lead to another . . . An unnerving flash of arousal convinced Emily she had better get out of there in a hurry.

"I . . . I have to go, David. I've got a ton of work at home. and I . . . I've got calls to make. And . . . I promised myself a facial." As she was tossing off inane excuses, she started to turn away from David only to collide with George. Or, more to the point, with the glass of champagne in George's left hand.

She let out a little cry as the drink spilled right down the front of her red dress.

George apologized profusely as she shook off his attempts to offer assistance and used the accident as an excuse to make her escape.

"I guess she must have really been nuts about that red dress," George mused as he looked over at David. "She did look hot in it." He eyed his young friend. "So, what do you think?"

"I think I have to go," David mumbled.

As Emily stumbled out of the house, she ran smack-dab into Liza and Chris. Now she felt completely unhinged. Not that the newlyweds seemed to notice Emily's frazzled state. Liza gave her an effusive hug while Chris gave her his trademark wink — the one he always used at the end of his broadcasts when he said good-night to all his faithful viewers. Was that really all she was to him?

Liza began prattling on about their move. "I've been telling Chris for ages that New York is *the* place to be. Can you believe he almost turned the offer down?"

Emily's eyes fixed on Chris. He looked incredibly handsome tonight in his black silk shirt and exquisite custom-tailored gray suit. It ought to be illegal for anyone to look that good. "You did?" Maybe he didn't want to leave L.A., after all. Maybe he didn't want to sever all his old ties. . . .

Chris ruffled Liza's flowing, dark locks. "I didn't almost turn it down. I just wanted the big boys upstairs to think I was almost turning it down. Did they or did they not jack up the offer, my love? And aren't I worth every extra penny?"

Liza slipped her arms around her husband's neck, a provocative smile playing on her lips. "And then some, darling."

He pulled her to him, wrapping his arms around her slender waist.

Emily felt her insides twist as she stood there in the street, watching the man she was desperately in love with embrace his wife. Damn! If only that old cliché, "Out of sight, out of mind," could be true. One thing was true: If she didn't get out of sight this instant, she might go out of her mind.

She started to turn away, when Liza's hand managed to uncoil from her husband's neck and snap around her forearm. "Look who's here," Liza said brightly, her gaze focused over Emily's shoulder.

Even before Emily glanced around, she knew it was David. Never again, she vowed, would she pinch-hit for her boss at a dumb cocktail party.

"How marvelous to bump into you, darling." Still clutching Emily's arm, Liza took hold of David's sleeve. "Do you know Emily? Oh, of course, you do. You two met at the wedding."

"Briefly," David mumbled, avoiding Emily's face. Not that he had to worry. She wasn't looking at him, either.

"Chris, do you know what we have to do?" Liza crooned.

Chris seductively placed both his hands on his wife's waist, a gesture neither David nor Emily failed to notice. "What do we have to do, dearest?" he teased playfully.

"We simply must have David and Emily over for dinner one night before we leave for New York."

The color—what little there was left of it—drained from both their faces.

"Oh, well, you'll probably be awfully busy getting ready for the move," Emily said hurriedly. "Maybe we can just get together for lunch one day, the two of us."

"And my schedule's really tight over the next few weeks," David quickly added. "I've got a shoot down in La Jolla in a few days. Then I've got to go up to San Francisco next week."

Emily gave David a sharp look. San Francisco next week? She prayed he wasn't going there for the Renée Lazar fashion show that she was going to be attending for *Chic*. She had the sinking feeling, now that she knew they were both in the same business, that their paths might cross far more than she had ever imagined. Far more than she was prepared for.

"We're not leaving for another month. We'll get around to it one of these nights," Liza said firmly, raising her hand to ward off any further possible protests or excuses. "And I won't take no for an answer."

Chris grinned. "She's a hard woman to turn down. Believe me, I know."

David and Emily knew it, too.

Oblivious to their mutual distress, Liza beamed at them. "Something tells me, the two of you might hit it off."

THEY WERE LEFT ALONE together as Liza bustled Chris off to the party, and stood there in silence for several moments.

"She probably won't get around to that dinner invitation. If she does . . . I'll get out of it," David offered gallantly.

"No. You go. I'll come down with a migraine." Emily could feel a headache starting already.

"I don't want to go," David said stubbornly. "Being around them . . . Well . . ."

"I know," Emily said quietly. "They're so . . ."

"Exactly."

"Maybe it's just as well that they're going to New York."

"I suppose."

She dug in her clutch bag for her car keys.

A half smile played on his lips. "You can have a migraine and I can come down with a cold."

Emily glanced at him, a little sparkle in her eyes. "With a fever?"

"A high fever." Oddly enough, he was feeling a bit feverish already.

Emily abruptly stuck her hand out. "It was nice seeing you again, David." They shook hands formally, both feeling more than a little foolish.

She started for her car, which she'd had to park halfway down the street. Just her luck, David had parked in the same direction. There was nothing for it but to walk to their cars together.

"How do you like working at *Chic?*" David asked in an effort to make small talk.

"Oh, it's very interesting." Emily gave a little laugh. "I came out here hoping to get a job on a news magazine. I was in the running for *L.A. Beat,* but someone 'beat' me out in the end. Then I heard about an opening at *Chic.* To be honest, I'd always considered fashion rags sort of . . . frivolous. However, a gal's got to eat and keep a roof over her head. And I do love the nitty-gritty work of putting a magazine together."

"It's a very-well-put-together magazine." It wasn't the magazine he was thinking about. It was Emily.

"How about you? Do you like being a fashion photographer?"

"Oh, yeah. It's very . . . interesting." He laughed dryly. "Actually, once upon a time I thought about growing up to be a photojournalist. Then . . . fashion . . . snatched my interest."

Fashion or a particular fashion designer? Emily wondered, knowing the answer. *The things we do for love. And look where it's gotten us.*

Emily was at her car. "Well . . ." She started to stretch out her hand, but changed her mind. She didn't want him to get the wrong idea, and think she was overly interested in making physical contact. She wasn't. Was she?

"Take care, David." She was careful not to in any way suggest that she might want to hear from him again. What was the point? Except to compare agonies. Like two patients thrown together in a semiprivate hospital room. Then again, she could almost hear her mother say, *Misery does love company.*

"You take care, too," David mumbled. Chalking up their one night of intimacy to mutual grief and loneliness, David was convinced that Emily wasn't his type. Not any more than he imagined he was hers.

Even though they'd said their goodbyes, they both hesitated, neither of them wanting to examine why.

"It's too bad about your dress."

"My dress?"

"The champagne."

"Oh. Oh, it doesn't matter. I don't really like this dress anyway."

"Really? You look . . . great in it."

"Thank you." She stifled the urge to add, *But I know you're just saying that.*

"ARE YOU GOING TO EAT that last slice?"

Emily gave her friend Cheryl a distracted shake of the head as they sat at a small marble-topped table in a bright, neon-lit trattoria near work.

Cheryl Quinn was an associate editor at *Chic,* one of the few women there who, like herself, didn't spend all her time and money trying to look like she just stepped out of the magazine. Cheryl was a sweet, plump woman in her early thirties with curly red hair, a quick smile and a warm heart. Emily had liked her instantaneously upon meeting her and the two had become good friends over the past couple of years.

"I envy you, Emily," Cheryl said, snatching up the piece of pizza before her friend changed her mind. "You have amazing willpower. I would kill for a body like yours. As long as I didn't have to work at it. Or give up pizza, Mexican food, and chocolate-crunch ice cream."

"You want to know my secret?"

Cheryl grinned. "I know your secret, Emily. I also don't want to have to be miserable and depressed because the guy I've been nuts about for umpteen years dumped me for a bimbo."

"Liza's not a bimbo."

Cheryl shrugged. "I know. I thought I might make you feel a little better if I called her one."

Emily managed a half smile. "And Chris didn't dump me. I wish he *had* dumped me."

Cheryl gave Emily a baffled look as she munched on her pizza.

"To be dumped implies that there was something going on before the dumping."

Cheryl smiled crookedly. "Better to have been loved and dumped than never to have been dumped at all?"

"Something like that."

"Well, if you want to get dumped, there's always hope. If not by Chris, then maybe you'll get lucky and meet someone else who might be an even better dumper."

"Very funny."

"Okay, the point is, you need to start going out, Emily. Maybe you'll discover that there is love after Chris Anders."

"I've had it with love, Cheryl. And I don't want to just . . . latch on to someone on the rebound. That would be an absolute disaster. It would be just . . . crazy. Dumb. Self-defeating." Her fingers played with her paper napkin. She looked across the booth at Cheryl, who was smiling. "What?"

Cheryl's brown eyes sparkled. "Why, Emily Bauer, you old devil, you met someone." Her eyes narrowed. "And you didn't even tell me."

Emily pressed her lips together, hating herself for being so transparent and feeling guilty for not having confided in her best friend. As close as she felt to Cheryl, she had been unable to bring herself to tell her about David. Too embarrassing? Too shameful? Too obvious?

"Look, if you don't want to talk about it . . ."

"It's not that," Emily said, her voice strained. "Well, it is that, but . . ."

"You're confused."

"No." Emily sighed. "Yes."

"Well, that's a start."

"I met him at the wedding."

"What's he like?"

"Nothing at all like Chris," Emily said.

Cheryl smiled. "If you ask me, that's a plus."

"He's in love with Liza."

"Chris?"

"David. The guy I met there."

"Not a plus."

"He took me home after the wedding. And...one thing led to another...." Emily could feel a hot flush rise to her cheeks.

Cheryl arched her brows. "A possible plus. How was he?"

Emily was aghast. "Cheryl, I threw myself at a man I didn't even know." She paused. "Well, he threw himself at me, too."

"So, you started off on an equal footing. A definite plus."

"Be serious, Cheryl. I'm mortified about what I...we did. And so is David. When I saw him last night we couldn't even look each other straight in the eye."

"Oh, so you saw him again."

"Purely by accident."

"You mean, he didn't call you after . . ."

"No. No, I didn't expect him to. I didn't want him to. We both felt . . . Don't you see? We were using each other."

"You mean you were two wounded souls looking for comfort and found it in each other's arms."

"You are such a romantic, Cheryl," Emily said morosely. "We were two jerks, looking for all the wrong things in all the wrong places."

Cheryl smiled sagely. "Sometimes, the places you think are wrong are the right ones. And vice versa."

Emily rolled her eyes.

"So, what does he look like? Is he a hunk?"

Emily didn't answer.

"A semihunk?"

"He reminds me of Jimmy Stewart."

"The geek in copyediting?"

"The actor."

"Isn't he kind of old?"

"I mean when he was younger. Much younger."

Cheryl nibbled on the crust of her pizza. "Let's see. The young Jimmy Stewart type. So that would make him tall, thin, kind of cute, earnest, a little goofy."

"He isn't at all goofy."

"Jimmy Stewart?"

"David Turner."

Emily grinned. "Definitely a plus."

"SHE LOOKED TERRIFIC."

Alan motioned the bartender to bring over another couple of beers. "You already told me that. Ten times."

"I wasn't expecting to see her," David said. "When I saw her, I almost lost it."

"You told me that, too."

"She was wearing this dress that . . ."

"David, you're making yourself crazy."

"I know."

"You're making me crazy."

"Sorry. It's just that every time I see Liza, something comes over me."

"Lust?"

"No. Well . . . yes. Only, it's more than that. I don't think Chris is capable of understanding her."

"She's not that hard to understand," Alan said dryly.

David scowled. "You never understood her, either. You only saw the woman she presented on the surface, not the real woman underneath."

The bartender arrived and deposited one beer in front of David, the other in front of Alan, sweeping away their empty glasses.

David stared at the refill. "How many does this make?"

Alan grinned. "Two."

"Did I tell you she invited us over for dinner?"

"Us?"

David's mouth twitched. "Me. Invited *me*."

Alan eyed him thoughtfully. Then he snapped his fingers. "Emily."

David looked at him, astounded. "How the hell did you . . . ?"

"It's this special look that comes over your face, Davey. A special Emily look."

"You're crazy."

"Crazy as a fox. So you did go out with that hot little number from the wedding again. I had a feeling—"

"Will you stop calling her a hot little number. I didn't go out with her again. We . . . ran into each other."

"Aha."

"She's an editor at a fashion magazine. The cocktail party was for a fashion designer. So we were both there. And Liza and Chris showed up. And we just happened to be standing near each other. Outside. Emily was leaving. And then I was leaving."

"You weren't leaving together."

"No," David said sharply. "We most certainly weren't leaving together. We met up outside because Liza and Chris had arrived and they were talking to Emily. We all sort of chatted for a few minutes." David lifted his beer glass and swallowed a good third of it down.

"And then?"

"And then we stopped chatting."

"And?"

"And we went our separate ways." He glanced over at Alan. "I know what you're trying to do."

"What am I trying to do?"

"You're trying to get me interested in Emily so I'll get my mind off Liza."

"Why should I do that? For all I know, this Emily's a dog."

"She most certainly is not a dog. What kind of way is that to talk about a woman? Emily happens to be extremely attractive and she has a very appealing personality. She's bright, funny, honest— What are you smiling at?"

"I was thinking that if I did want to try to get you interested in Emily, I wouldn't have to try very hard."

David scowled, then chugalugged the rest of his beer.

. . . I was thinking th . . .

4

"GHASTLY. ABSOLUTELY ghastly," Naomi Bauer muttered, much to her daughter's consternation. Why, Emily asked herself, had she ever agreed to bring her mother up to San Francisco for the Lazar fashion show?

"Please keep your comments to yourself," Emily pleaded as they settled in for a ten-minute break. "Someone might hear you."

Emily glanced nervously around the crowded room, on the lookout for David Turner. So far, so good. The show was half over and she hadn't seen any sign of him. Maybe his trip to San Francisco had nothing to do with the show. Maybe he had other business here. Or pleasure?

"Don't frown, Emily. It'll make tiny little crease marks across the bridge of your nose that will never go away."

"I wasn't frowning. I was thinking."

Emily not only wished she hadn't brought her mother along, she wished she hadn't come herself. She was too edgy, too nervous. It was dumb. David Turner wasn't here. She could relax. This time, anyway.

Yet it was inevitable that she would run into him again. At another cocktail party. A fashion show. A shoot. Even at *Chic*. There was only so much maneuvering either one of them was going to be able to do to avoid each other.

"Really, Emily, who in their right mind would mix organdy with polyester? The revamping of the leisure suit. It will never take hold. Never."

Emily had to agree with her mother, for once. The Lazar collection was truly dreadful. Especially the designer's leisure suits.

"There's never anything new in fashion, Mother. Things just sort of get reshuffled around. Anyway, Lazar's company is a major advertiser in *Chic* and as a representative of the magazine I'm expected to treat her and her leisure suits or whatever, with kid gloves."

"Do you want me to gush and drool over her collection when you introduce me to her after the show?"

"You don't have to drool. In fact, you don't have to meet her. I'll only be with her for a few minutes and you can wait for me—"

"And miss an opportunity to meet a famous celebrity like Renée Lazar in the flesh? You know how I adore celebrities, Emily. There's this amazing energy and magnetism that positively radiates from them. Take Chris...."

Emily closed her eyes. "Not again, Mother."

Naomi Bauer shrugged. "Have you seen him?"

"Do you want me to get you something from the bar before the show starts again?"

"No."

Emily rose. "Well, I think I'll get myself a club soda."

"You're not fooling me one bit, Emily."

"I know, Mother. I gave up trying long ago."

"Emily."

She almost dropped the glass of club soda in her hand as she heard the sound of what was becoming an all-too-familiar voice. "David."

Their eyes met in the mirror over the bar. The man standing between them stepped away with a smile. He was the only one of the three smiling.

David's gaze shifted nervously from the mirror to Emily in the flesh. "I didn't . . . see you here."

Emily gave an ambiguous wave, spilling some of her club soda. She pretended not to notice. "I'm over there. Toward the front."

"I've got a seat in back. I got here late. A bomb threat on my plane up from L.A."

"Oh, that's terrible."

"They didn't find any bomb."

"Well, that's a relief, anyway."

"The plane was held up for over an hour, though, while they went through it with a fine-tooth comb."

"That's . . . too bad."

"Yes."

"I guess it's better than if . . . they'd found a bomb."

"Yes."

"I don't like flying."

"I don't usually mind. Except for the delays."

"Bomb threats and such."

David nodded.

"Well . . . I guess I'd better get back to my seat." She started to turn away.

David knew all he had to do was nod again and the encounter would be over. Instead, he heard himself say, "How's the show so far?"

Emily turned back, smiling for the first time. "Ghastly. Absolutely ghastly."

David found himself thinking that Emily Bauer had a very disarming smile. Or maybe he was simply in a mood to be disarmed. "What's she into, this time around?"

"Are you ready?" She leaned a little closer, giving him a conspiratorial look, but David was more aware of her lavender-scented perfume than her expression. "Unisex polyester leisure suits."

They both laughed, and for a moment each of them relaxed just a little.

"Let's make a pact never to wear one," David said with mock solemnity.

"Never."

David extended his hand. Emily hesitated for a moment, then followed suit. Their hands were engaged in a quasi shake cum grasp when Emily heard another familiar voice over her shoulder.

"So, are you going to introduce me?"

Emily automatically drew her hand away from David's. "Oh . . . Mother. This is—" Suddenly her mind went blank. David filled in the blank.

"David Turner."

"Naomi Bauer. Emily's mother."

"Nice to meet you, Mrs. Bauer."

"Naomi, please. I hate formality. Besides, it makes me feel so old to be called Mrs. Bauer. And actually, now that Mr. Bauer and I are divorced it feels rather bogus to be called Mrs. Bauer. I've even contemplated going back to my maiden name. Samuelson. Only I think it might be awkward for Emily. Maybe once she's married. Then again, she might not take her husband's name. Women often don't, these days. Although, somehow I always thought Emily would. Especially if it was a certain last name. . . ."

A flush flared in Emily's cheeks—a mixture of embarrassment and anger. "The show's starting, Mother," she said tightly. "We really must get back to our seats."

"Well, it was nice meeting you, David," Naomi said, extending her hand and giving his hand a firm shake.

"Same here, Naomi."

"Are you a designer?"

"No. He's a photographer," Emily said, gripping her mother's arm. "Please, Mother. We have to get back to our seats."

Naomi smiled at David. "I didn't think you were a designer.

"HE'S NOT FOR YOU, Emily," Naomi announced as soon as they'd settled into their seats.

"I don't know what you're talking about."

"Oh, he seems perfectly nice. He's got good teeth, healthy skin, pleasant features. But he doesn't have that . . . that special dynamism. There's just no charisma. No oomph. The one thing I worry about the most since Chris got married is that you'll end up just settling for someone . . . ordinary."

"David isn't ordinary," Emily snapped, then immediately regretted her words as she saw the bemused look on her mother's face.

"I mean," she went on, "you can't go around classifying men—people—that way. Not without even knowing them."

"So, you know David well?"

"Shh. They're about to start." Never had Emily so looked forward to a continuation of a fashion show—ghastly leisure suits notwithstanding.

"THIS IS THE FIRST TIME in nearly six weeks that we've had ourselves a good workout," Alan said as he and David walked off the squash court. "I hope this means you've finally stopped moping about Liza's move east."

David gave Alan a noncommittal look.

Alan smiled. "Say, since you beat me today, how about you buy lunch?"

David hesitated. "Sorry. I can't make lunch today. How about a rain check? Next week?"

Alan shot his friend a shrewd look. "Got a hot date?"

David sighed. "You don't give up, do you?"

"Just curious. I think it's great if you're starting to date again, get back into the swing of things.... Well, not that you ever really were exactly in the swing of things, but ..."

"I'm going to New York."

Alan stopped short. "To see Liza?"

"I've got a shoot there...."

"So, that's why you're so up. Why you beat the pants off of me. And here I thought ..."

"You think too much. I told you I'm going there on business."

"And you're not going to see Liza?" Alan prodded.

"Okay, okay. We'll probably meet for lunch. We never did manage to get together before she left L.A. Neither one of us could seem to work it into our schedules."

"Then there was Emily. Didn't you tell me that Liza was planning to have the two of you over for dinner? I guess that would have been kind of awkward."

"Honestly, Alan. Emily and I are both mature people. We would have ... handled it in a ... mature way." David didn't elucidate.

They stepped out into the parking lot behind the health club. "So, who invited who to lunch in The Big Apple?" Alan asked, walking along with David as he headed for his car.

"What difference does that make? We just want to ... to touch base, catch up with each other. I'm going to be there anyway, and ..."

"You asked her."

David scowled. "Don't go making this into something it isn't. She's a married woman. And I'm ... an old friend."

"David, David ..."

"I'm not harboring any fantasies about the two of us."

"Baloney." Alan never was one to pull any punches. "You're hoping she'll walk into that restaurant, confess to you that she made the biggest mistake of her life choosing Chris over you. You're hoping she'll divorce him, marry you and the two of you will get to live happily ever after, after all."

"You're nuts. Are you finished?" David asked tightly, pulling open his car door.

"I'm finished," Alan said soberly. "The question is, when is this going to be finished for you?"

DAVID ARRIVED AT THE bustling bistro in midtown Manhattan ten minutes early. He plucked the fan-folded, burnt umber linen napkin from the table and spread it over his lap, then thought better of it, and tried to reshape it and return it to its proper spot behind the teal-blue plate. The napkin sagged against the water glass. He fussed with it for a few minutes, gave up, and returned it to his lap.

To placate the waitress who kept coming over every five minutes asking him if he'd like to order now, David ordered first one glass of wine, then a second. . . .

He was on his third glass of well-chilled Chardonnay when Liza showed up, a half-hour late. He sucked in a slow breath and rose from his chair. She was wearing a vibrant red cotton dress and, for a moment, David's mind flashed to another red dress, another woman. . . .

"You're staring. Is my slip showing?" Liza had a breathy voice that made David forget everything he was thinking.

He smiled crookedly, realizing that he was slightly tipsy — in a good way. "What man in his right mind wouldn't stare at you?"

Liza trilled a laugh as she slid into the chair across from him. "That's what I love about you, David."

His smile took on a soulful cast.

"Are you all right?"

"Sure," David said. "Why?"

"Because you're still standing."

Embarrassed, he instantly sat down.

With quick efficiency, Liza picked up the menu, gave it a glance, then motioned to the waitress. "Chef's salad, vinaigrette dressing on the side. No onions or olives. Extra sprouts. And a glass of mineral water with a lime."

David, his gaze locked on a stray tendril of Liza's hair that fell provocatively over one eye, had to be asked twice by the waitress if he knew what he wanted.

Pulling his eyes away from Liza, he looked up at the impatient waitress. He knew what he wanted, all right. Unfortunately, it wasn't on the menu.

"I'll have what she's having," he muttered distractedly.

After the waitress took off, Liza reached her hand across the small table and took hold of David's sleeve. "It's so good to see you."

"Is it?"

She gave him a pouty look. "You're not mad at me for not coming through with that dinner invitation before I left L.A.? Or for having to turn down all those sweet lunch invites from you? Things were just so crazy. And Chris was driving me up a tree."

David brightened. "He was?"

Her expression turned intimate, setting off feelings inside him he'd forgotten were there. "He's impossible. Completely impossible."

"He is?" Expectation hung in the smoke-filled air.

Liza flashed a wide smile. "It's a good thing he's so gorgeous and so damned irresistible." She smiled coyly. "And it's a good thing he knows how lucky he is to have me."

David saw his hopes—the very ones Alan had verbalized and he'd denied—fly right out of the bistro.

For the next half-hour, while he tried to work his way through a chef's salad with extra sprouts—he hated sprouts, he hated chef's salads—Liza regaled him with tales of marital bliss and the marvelous career opportunities that were coming her way. It wasn't until the waitress had carted off their oversize glass dishes at the end of the meal that Liza thought to ask David how his life was going.

"Well, pretty much the same. Fine, really. Busy."

"How's your pal and my old flame, Alan, doing? I suppose the divorce business is booming as ever."

David shrugged. "I suppose."

"I can't understand why so many couples can't be happy, David. Why so many marriages fail."

David gave her a level look. "Sometimes people make the wrong choice."

Liza shook her head. "I know what the real problem is. Most people don't know themselves? They don't know who they are and what they need. They lack insight and judgment."

David fiddled with his teaspoon. "I imagine most people think they know themselves, think they've picked the right person for them. Only...sometimes they later realize they've ... made a mistake in judgment."

Liza sighed. "I'm one of the lucky ones, then. I know that Chris and I are perfectly matched. I knew it practically the moment I set eyes on him. And he felt the same way. It was magic. Pure magic. We speak the same language. We have so much in common—drive, ambition, determination, sincerity. Oh, things are more hectic and pressured for us here than they were in L.A., but we're playing in the big leagues now."

She went on to tell him about their mad social whirl, dropping famous names, telling little "in" jokes that David didn't really get.

Finally, after a quick check of her watch, she reached across and squeezed David's hand. "This is awful of me. I've done almost all of the talking and now I've got to run. You do look great, David. And I'm so glad things are going well for you. And that you're happy. You are happy, aren't you?"

What could he say? "I'm happy that you're happy, Liza," he murmured softly, doubtful that she'd heard him as she gathered up her tote bag and rose.

"Next lunch is on me," she said brightly, bussing David on the cheek and then hurrying off.

The minute she left, he fell into a depression. *Next lunch is on me*. When was the next lunch likely to be?

"I'M TELLING YOU I SAW him," Cheryl announced as she entered Emily's office and sat down in a chair in front of the desk.

Emily stared at her in disbelief. "Getting into a cab?"

"In front of the Beverly Hilton."

"On Wilshire?"

Cheryl nodded.

"This morning?"

"Emily, I'm telling you, Chris Anders is in town. I mean, no big deal, right? You're not still carrying a torch for the guy now that he's an old married man?"

"Two months isn't an old married man. And no, I'm not still carrying a torch for him." Emily couldn't quite meet Cheryl's all-too-shrewd eyes. "It's just that, if it is him, I'd have thought he might give me a buzz. For old time's sake. We have known each other practically our whole lives. I mean, we have a history."

"A history," Cheryl repeated without inflection.

"Okay, so it wasn't a torrid history. Still . . ." Emily left the sentence hanging, shifting to another one. "Maybe it was someone who looked like Chris."

"Isn't he one of a kind?" Cheryl said glibly, plucking the receiver of the telephone from its cradle on Emily's desk.

Emily stared at the receiver.

"Go on. Call the Beverly Hilton and ask if they've got a Chris Anders registered there."

Emily made no move.

"Okay, I'll call."

Emily snatched the phone away from Cheryl. "This is ridiculous," she muttered, coming up with the number for the hotel on her Rolodex.

A minute later as Emily hung up the phone, her facial muscles went slack. "He's there."

"I'm sorry, Emily," Cheryl said softly. "Most likely he just flew in and—"

"He's been there for five days."

Cheryl made no response.

"It doesn't matter," she mumbled, relieved that Cheryl made a graceful exit without offering any useless platitudes.

An hour later, having gotten absolutely no work done, Emily redialed the Hilton, but aborted the call before it started ringing.

Twenty minutes later, she dialed again.

EVERY TIME SOMEONE entered the bar at the hotel, Emily looked over expectantly. By six-fifteen, she began to give up hope. Maybe he hadn't picked up his message. Maybe he was tied up in meetings. Maybe he'd gotten struck by a truck crossing the street. Maybe . . . he just didn't care.

The thought vanished in a flash. There he was. Walking into the bar. His larger-than-life presence seemed to fill up the whole room. Emily was well aware hers weren't the only eyes on Chris. He was like a bright flame that drew every moth in sight.

He looked fantastic. Better than ever. Emily wasn't surprised that success agreed with him. She refused to give his marriage any credit.

As he caught her eye, smiled, and started over to her table, Emily was filled with a familiar longing. Now it was more mournful than sexual.

He came to a stop a few feet from her, wearing his sheepish smile almost as well as he wore his perfectly tailored business suit.

"I was planning to call you. You beat me to it."

She smiled. Okay, so she wanted to believe him. He was a man who liked to do things in his own sweet time.

He sat down. "What are you drinking?"

"White wine. Chardonnay, I think."

He motioned to the waitress and ordered a Scotch on the rocks.

"What are you doing back in L.A.?" Emily asked.

"As part of the deal for being let out of my contract early, I agreed to host a one-hour special on the Lakers. I did most of the prep work in New York and we're taping it here this week."

"And Liza? How come she didn't join you?" Thanks to a chatty desk clerk who was an avid Chris Anders fan, Emily had found out earlier that he had checked in sans wife.

"She couldn't get away. Her designs are really taking off. She's thinking about starting her own company. House of Liza. Hey, maybe *Chic* will fly you east to interview her. Liza would get a kick out of seeing you."

"Oh, I feel the same," Emily lied, taking a sip of wine.

When the waitress brought over his drink, she smiled shyly at him. "Aren't you . . . Chris Anders?"

He flashed the pretty young blonde one of his infamous smiles. "In the flesh."

Not only did he end up giving her his autograph, but also the two other ogling waitresses on duty. After five minutes of fawning all over him, the three entranced women were finally shooed off by the maitre d'.

"Fame certainly agrees with you," Emily said, a touch ruefully.

"It's a gas, Em. Now that I've gone national, people recognize me when I'm in a bar in New York, L.A., Houston, Cincinnati, Timbuktu."

"You'd better be careful or I'm going to start thinking you're hanging out in a lot of bars," Emily remarked sardonically.

Chris grinned. "You know what I mean."

"I know what you mean."

"Not that there isn't a lot more pressure, more expectations, more responsibilities. The payoff is worth it. Not only career-wise. Liza eats up all the glamour as much as I do. With both of us making names for ourselves, we're moving right into the A list. The people we meet. It would make your head swim, Em."

"I'm sure."

A grin edged on to his handsome face. "Let me tell ya, babe, life at the top ain't half bad."

"And that includes married life . . . ?" Emily could kick herself, but the question had just slipped out. Maybe she was a masochist at heart.

He took a swallow of his drink before answering. "We have terrific fights."

Emily was confused. "Terrific?"

He laughed. "Neither one of us is shy when it comes to expressing ourselves. We have these slam-bang clashes. Yelling, screaming, throwing things. Well, Liza throws. I catch. She's one fiery little wench. God, is she beautiful when she's angry. Half the time I think she blows up because she knows it turns me on. It's true, Em."

"I wasn't going to contest it," she said dryly, wishing now she'd never suggested this torturous get-together. Why couldn't she learn to leave well enough alone? Even if it wasn't all that *well!*

"I'm crazy about her, Em. She keeps me on my toes. Every guy who meets her is jealous as hell of me. Of course," he added, "she says the same is true about the women who meet me." He attempted a modest smile, but modesty just wasn't part of Chris Anders's repertoire. Emily had given up holding this against him long ago. She knew his faults. Who didn't have faults? At least, on Chris, they looked good.

"Say, what do I hear about you and David Turner?"

Emily did a double take. She could feel the heat spreading over her cheeks. "David . . . Turner?"

"Yeah. Liza hears the two of you are an item."

"David told Liza that we were an item?" Emily was incredulous. For one thing, it certainly wasn't true. She hadn't even bumped into him in weeks. For another thing, she couldn't imagine David telling Liza, the love of his life, any such lie.

"No, I don't think it was David who told her. I think it was one of David's pals, Alan Freese. He dropped her a note a week or so ago."

"I don't know Alan Freese, but he's got the story wrong," Emily said adamantly. "I hardly...know David." She was glad the dim lighting in the bar kept Chris from seeing her flush. Then again, knowing Chris, he wouldn't have noticed.

"Liza says he's a terrific guy. Sensitive, thoughtful, generous, smart. She was real happy to hear that the two of you were seeing each other. In fact, it had been her idea to try to get the two of you together."

"We're not together."

"Liza told me that David used to have a big crush on her, and she was kind of relieved that he'd finally found someone...."

"He hasn't found someone," she said, increasingly frustrated as Chris continued to ignore her denials.

"I think it's great, too, Em. Really, I do. All these years we've known each other, I've never really seen you get serious about any guy. It's about time. I'll tell you, Em. There's nothing like being in love. Take it from me."

Was he blind as well as deaf? Did he really have no idea how much she had loved him all these years? And what about Liza? How could she sum up David's heartfelt love and adoration for her as nothing more than a big crush? He'd certainly be 'crushed' if he knew. Emily felt irritated with Chris, surprisingly defensive and protective of David.

"David happens to be a man with deep feelings, Chris." She was glad he didn't ask her how she happened to know that, at the same time claiming to hardly know him. "Furthermore, he and I are not an item. I'm not..."

"It takes two to tango, Em. You've got to give a little to get a little." He broke out in a wide smile. "Say, that would make a good line for a song."

"I think it already is a line."

Chris finished up his drink, then rubbed his hands together. "Well, it's back to the grindstone."

"You're working tonight? I thought we might have dinner...." There was no hiding the disappointment in her voice. It even got through to Chris.

"Sorry, Em. I would have loved to make a night of it, catch up on the latest news and all, but we've got to wrap up taping tonight. I'm flying out first thing tomorrow morning."

She stared at him in disbelief. "Tomorrow morning?" Exactly when had he been planning to call her? From the airport?

He was on his feet, slapping a large bill on the table. "This was really fun. Say, next time we're in town—Liza and I—we'll take you and David out to dinner. We'll go to Spago's. This time you can bet your bottom dollar the maitre d' won't stick me at some back table. This time we'll be part of the celebrity buzz. What do you say? The four of us."

He was already squeezing her shoulder and starting off when Emily mumbled wearily, "David and I aren't dating."

As she watched Chris make his sweeping exit, stopping briefly to give a regal wave to the three waitresses, Emily acknowledged that this truly had been a bad idea.

TWO NIGHTS LATER, Emily and Cheryl were having dinner at a small Chinese restaurant near Emily's apartment. While Emily was busy spooning out her Shanghai chicken, Cheryl's eyes kept darting across the room, a thoughtful expression on her face.

"Don't you want any of this?" Emily asked. Then, seeing that her friend was distracted, she gave her a puzzled look. "What's the matter? Don't tell me. Chris just walked into the restaurant. Well, this time I know you're wrong. He flew out of LAX yesterday morning."

Cheryl pursed her lips together. "No, it's not Chris. However, there is a guy across the way who keeps looking—" She stopped abruptly, snapping her fingers. "What a ninny."

"The guy?"

Cheryl grinned. "Me. I should have realized. It's Jimmy Stewart. A young Jimmy Stewart. You're right. He doesn't look goofy. He looks kind of cute. Very cute. And his dinner partner isn't half bad either," Cheryl joked.

Emily blanched. "His dinner partner?"

"Yeah, a luscious blonde. What a body."

Emily felt a disconcerting twinge of jealousy. The feeling confused her. Did she think David should remain loyal to Liza even though Liza was married? Or did she have some crazy idea that he should remain loyal to her? Now, that *was* crazy.

"He keeps looking this way. So does the blonde."

There was no way Emily could resist glancing around. The minute she did, she made eye contact with David. And with the blond. Emily managed a quick, awkward smile and a meager attempt at a wave, then she turned back to Cheryl, eyes glinting. "A luscious blond."

Cheryl grinned. "Well, he is blond. And he is luscious. The question is, is he taken?"

"I wouldn't know. I have no idea who he is."

"Well, we're about to find out."

"What do you mean?"

"He's coming over to our table."

"Alone?"

Before Cheryl had the chance to respond, the attractive, ruggedly built blond-haired man was at Emily's side, extending his hand to her. "I'm Alan. And you're Emily."

Disconcerted, Emily shook his hand. Alan. Was this the same Alan who had dropped Liza the note about her and David being an item? She glanced back at David, her cheeks flushed. He gave her a small smile.

Cheryl's arm darted out. "I'm Cheryl."

Alan smiled, taking Cheryl's hand in turn. Then he glanced at the Shanghai chicken and the as-yet-untouched sweet-and-sour shrimp. "Say, I have a great idea. Why don't we pool your chicken and shrimp with our beef-and-broccoli and pork Lo Mein and have ourselves a real Chinese feast?"

Again, Emily glanced nervously back at David, who was now sitting very still and expressionless at his table.

"Oh, it was David's idea," Alan said cheerily, scooping up one of the dishes, Cheryl eagerly scooping up the other.

Emily was slower to make a move.

"Why don't you bring over the rice?" Cheryl called out brightly.

"THE BEST LO MEIN I ever tasted," Alan said with a sated smile at the end of the meal.

"I think the Shanghai chicken could have been a little spicier," Cheryl remarked. "I absolutely adored the beef-and-broccoli." She looked across at Emily. "Did you even try the beef?"

Emily nodded.

"What did you think of the beef, David?" Cheryl asked.

"What?"

"The beef-and-broccoli?"

"Oh. Good. Very good."

"You hardly touched it," Alan pointed out.

"I don't really like broccoli," David mumbled.

"You just said it was good," Cheryl pointed out.

"I did?"

"What about you, Emily? Do you like broccoli?"

"What?"

Cheryl grinned at Alan, who winked at her. While David and Emily had remained constrained and barely communicative throughout the "feast," their dinner partners had been having themselves a merry time getting acquainted.

The waiter cleared the table and brought over the fortune cookies. Cheryl opened hers first. She read aloud. "'You will meet a tall, handsome stranger who will sweep you off your feet.'" She crumpled it up with a little laugh in Alan's direction. "Or something like that."

Alan grinned, cracking open his cookie. "You will sweep a lovely young thing off her feet tonight." His grin widened as he, too, crumpled up his thin snippet of paper, his sparkling gaze falling on Cheryl.

Neither Emily nor David reached for a fortune cookie. Cheryl and Alan were not to be denied. Cheryl snapped one open for Emily, who snatched it from her before she could embellish what was written on the slip.

"Come on. You have to read it aloud," Alan prompted.

Emily hesitated. "All good things come to those who wait," she mumbled.

Cheryl and Alan clapped. "Patience pays," Cheryl re-phrased, giving her friend a nudge.

"Your turn, Davey."

David reluctantly picked up the last remaining fortune cookie and snapped it in half. After he pulled out the sliver of paper, he stared at it in consternation.

"So?" Cheryl prodded.

"Cat got your tongue?" Alan teased.

David shot Emily a glance. "It's the same."

Cheryl didn't get it. "That's the fortune?"

"Let me see," Alan said, snatching the slip from David, reading, then smiling. "All good things come to those who wait." His smile deepened as he looked from David to Emily. "Talk about coincidence."

OUTSIDE THE RESTAURANT Emily and David found them-selves quickly abandoned, Alan having offered Cheryl a lift home, which she quickly accepted, deliberately not men-tioning that she had her own car parked down the street.

"I guess they really hit it off," David said after the pair made their departure.

"I once saw a movie like this."

David stuck his hands in his pockets. "She seems very nice."

Emily gave him a quick glance. "He isn't married or any-thing?"

"Alan? No way. He's handled too many divorces to think very highly of marriage."

"Oh."

"Not that he's totally antimarriage. He's cautious."

"Nothing wrong with being cautious."

"Nothing wrong with it at all."

They started walking together down the street. Emily's apartment was just a few blocks away. David's was even closer.

When they got to the corner, Emily came to an abrupt stop. "David."

David stepped back up on the curb. "Yes, Emily?"

"I was just thinking...."

He nodded. He'd been doing some thinking, too.

"The thing is," she went on, "we're bound to keep crossing paths socially... professionally...."

He observed her closely. "It certainly seems that way."

"And I think you feel equally... awkward...."

"I suppose. A little."

"Isn't there some way we can...? What I mean is, I don't want—and I don't think you want—what... what happened between us that one night...to be a continuous source of... embarrassment to both of us...."

David smiled at her. "I agree."

"You do?" She was moved by his smile. It was so sensitive, thoughtful, generous....

"Absolutely."

She smiled back at him, clearly relieved, and they started walking again.

Halfway down the block, Emily said quietly, "I saw Chris the other day. He was in town. We had a drink together at his hotel. In the bar."

"How is he?"

"Oh, great. You know."

David's smile was tinged with sympathy.

They walked some more.

"I saw Liza when I was in New York a couple of weeks ago. We had lunch together."

Emily glanced at him.

He smiled, but the smile didn't touch his eyes. Emily didn't expect it would. "She's great, too." A brief pause. "They're both great." Another pause. "So, it's great."

Emily came to another stop and stared him down. "Not great."

He nodded. "Not great."

They turned the corner. David slowed as they approached a converted warehouse.

"Your place?"

David nodded, glancing at the building. "Want to come up for coffee? Some dessert?"

Emily hesitated, as a warning sign blinked on. And then, just as quickly, blinked off. Or was she just looking the other way? "Well, I guess we really can't count those fortune cookies as dessert."

David was already holding open the door for her.

5

"AND HE'S LOOKING SO happy...."

"And you're trying to look happy, too. Only inside, your heart is breaking."

"Exactly," Emily said, finishing off a slice of cinnamon crumb cake. "I knew you'd understand completely, David. You're the only person I feel I could really talk to about...all this."

"I feel the same way," David admitted, washing down his cake with a glass of cold milk. "There's no one else...."

"What about your friend, Alan?"

David shook his head, wiping his lips with his napkin. "Alan's the last person I'd talk to about . . . all this."

"Then how did he know about me?"

David frowned. "The man's a lawyer. Believe me, it wasn't voluntary. I didn't *tell* him anything. He surmised."

Emily nodded.

David looked across at her. "Alan used to date Liza."

Instinctively, Emily's hand reached out for David's as they sat across from each other at a small marble-topped ice-cream table in the kitchen area of his loft. "That's awful."

"It was pretty hard at the time. Let's face it. Liza has always gone for . . . flashy guys."

"Chris, too," Emily muttered gloomily. Then, when she saw David grin, she quickly added, "I mean, flashy women."

They both laughed. Then Emily grew serious.

"Was Alan madly in love with Liza?" she asked.

"He was madly in lust, anyway. Their relationship was very intense but thankfully brief."

"She dumped him?"

"Well, that's up for debate. Liza told me she dumped Alan, but Alan's story is he dumped her."

"Who do you believe?"

"To be honest, I sort of believe them both. I mean, I think they both wanted out at around the same time. And they each needed to see themselves as the—"

"Dumper and not the dumpee?"

David smiled. "Precisely."

They both grew silent.

"That isn't the only reason I don't talk to Alan about Liza." Emily waited.

"He's forever ribbing me as it is, about . . . well, about my feelings for her. He doesn't see Liza the way I do. His perspective is skewed. They may have had a brief affair, but he never really got to know Liza. He thinks I'm . . . cracked to keep on carrying this torch for her."

"Cheryl has the same attitude about my feelings for Chris."

"Were she and Chris ever . . . involved?"

"Oh, no. Nothing like that." There was a brief hesitation. "I'm sure they weren't."

"I just thought—"

"No."

Another silence fell.

"I suppose I am a little . . . cracked," David confessed.

A small smile curled Emily's lips. "I suppose I am, too." She shrugged. "I mean, what's the point?"

"Exactly."

Emily moved some crumbs around her plate. "The only problem is, love isn't like a faucet. You can't just shut it off when everything starts . . . overflowing, flooding, causing a big mess."

"It would be nice, though, wouldn't it. Turn a little knob and . . . zap."

Emily rose and started walking aimlessly about the loft. "I should never have gotten together with him the other evening. That was my big mistake. I was doing okay—not great, but okay—after he left." She glanced back at David. "You know. Out of sight, out of mind."

David nodded, rising. "I regretted that lunch with Liza practically from the moment she walked into the restaurant." He stopped, remembering how Emily had popped into his head when he'd first seen Liza. Then, as always in the past, Liza's presence—her smile, her voice, her mannerisms, everything about her—drove all thoughts of every other woman from his mind. Liza had spoiled him for other women—for all her faults. David was far from denying her flaws, but you didn't love someone because she was perfect.

"It was hard enough before he was married," Emily was saying, lost in her own private torment. "It always seemed like there was someone else in the picture. Someone beautiful, glamorous, talented, brimming with self-assurance. Yet, I held out hope. My mother almost had me convinced that in the end he would . . ." She had to fight back tears. "Only now . . ."

David was staring off into space. "I remember I felt sort of invisible while we sat there in that restaurant, Liza chattering away obliviously."

Emily turned to David, their gazes connecting. "Invisible. Yes, it was like that for me, too. Like I wasn't really there. Chris sort of took up all the space for both of us." She turned away abruptly.

David could see her shoulders heave. "Emily, are you crying?"

She kept her back to him, one hand darting to her face, the other waving him off. "Oh, just ignore me. It's nothing.

Honestly. You should have seen me the other night, after Chris left the bar. I could hardly see straight leaving the hotel, I was crying so hard. I'm sure everyone in the lobby was staring at me. I couldn't help it. It was like a dam had broken loose and I couldn't plug it back up. The doorman felt so sorry for me, he slipped the cabbie a ten-dollar bill and told me the ride was on him."

"I felt like crying after my lunch date with Liza," David confided.

Emily gave a little start as he spoke, realizing only now that he was right behind her.

"It's very nineties for men to cry," Emily murmured.

David gave a wry laugh. "The sensitive New Age man. That's me."

Emily turned around. Tears streaked down her cheeks but she was no longer crying. Their eyes locked.

Hers appeared to him suddenly larger, darker, almost magnetic. Maybe it was just that she'd been crying. Maybe it was the lighting in the room—an illusion. Despite his rationalizations, he felt captivated.

As their gazes continued to hold, Emily was struck not only by the warmth and clarity in David's eyes, but by the startling sensuality she suddenly saw in them. Like it or not, she felt a ripple of desire.

As the silence stretched, the long moment grew awkward. Their gazes faltered, each of them looking elsewhere. David focused on the mauve rug at his feet, studying its flat weave. Emily's eyes fell on a grouping of photos on a nearby wall. Surprise was etched on her features as she stepped closer to them.

"Did you take these?"

He gave a self-conscious shrug. "It's just a hobby. I told you, once upon a time I wanted to be a photojournalist."

"You certainly did," she said with newfound respect in her voice as she went from photo to photo. A shot of a fire ravaging a forest, and in the foreground a group of fire fighters, their faces covered in grime and tears. An overturned car on a riot-strewn L.A. street, a child nearby crying as she huddled against her frightened mother's skirt. A group of teenagers being carted into a police station by three policemen, frustration etched on the cops' faces, fear mingling with rage and pride on the faces of the youths.

She stared at David, seeing him as she never had before. "These are incredible. They're so powerful. What's even more remarkable, they're so…personal. You don't just capture an event. It's like you get into the heart and soul of the picture. Does that make sense? I can't really explain it."

"No one's ever explained it better."

They stared at each other, suddenly silent—a silence that was potent and intense.

"You're . . . very talented," she murmured.

"Thank you." David felt his body stirring, temptation playing havoc with his mind. *Don't go getting carried away. Don't make more of this than it is. You're just touched by her compliments. Flattered. And you're feeling lonely and hurt, like the last time. And so is Emily.* If things were awkward between them before, David knew they'd be almost impossible now. That was, if . . .

Emily could feel her heart racing. If she wasn't careful, they'd end up in bed again. Which, at the moment, she had to admit, was alarmingly tempting. This would only be a replay of their last intimate encounter, she warned herself. Once again they'd begun pouring their hearts out about Chris and Liza, feeling the pangs of disappointment, loss, sympathy. Those emotions were their only real bond. And Emily knew those emotions alone weren't strong enough by half to let them face the "morning after" without feeling even more embarrassed, humiliated and regretful than they had that other disastrous morning.

Detour before it's too late, Emily thought in a panic.

David, too, was thinking of an escape route.

They stepped away from each other at the same time.

"It's getting late," Emily said, her voice hoarse thanks to a suddenly dry throat.

"Right." David's voice was equally raspy.

She avoided looking at him; avoided looking at the photos that had stirred something so primal in her.

She walked to the door. Feeling the safety of distance, she flashed him a smile. "I suppose I'll be seeing you around."

"You're not going to walk?"

"It's only a few blocks."

"Nobody walks in L.A."

They both smiled.

"I'll walk you...."

"No," she said adamantly, desperate for some distance from David. "Thanks. Really, it's just a few blocks. Well, you know that anyway."

"It's not safe...."

"This is a safe neighborhood. Anyway, I took a course in self-defense. I was first in my class."

He smiled. "I'll keep that in mind."

"See you."

"See you."

NAOMI BAUER WAS BUSY rearranging the bouquet of flowers in Emily's glass vase. Emily had picked them up at a florist's near work, but hadn't had time to do more than pop them in water.

"Your father used to bring me daisies when we were first married. Then, when he started making money, roses. A dozen roses for absolutely no reason. I miss having flowers around the house."

Emily came over to her mother and put an arm around her shoulder. Even though she knew very well that it wasn't the roses her mother missed but her father, she murmured, "There's no law against buying yourself flowers."

"I suppose. Only it isn't the same thing."

"No, I suppose it isn't," she admitted. "It's still nice having flowers around the place."

Naomi shrugged, stepping away from the vase and from her daughter's light embrace. Emily understood. Her mother had a hard time accepting sympathy.

"I've noticed that Chris has been looking very pale lately."

Emily wasn't taken aback by her mother's abrupt mention of Chris. She'd been waiting for it. Invariably, Chris Anders managed to come up as a topic of conversation whenever she and her mother got together.

"Maybe your television set's going."

"That old spark in his eyes is missing. And it's not my television set."

Emily stepped into the kitchen to check on dinner. She was sorry now that they hadn't gone out to eat. She felt more vulnerable here alone in her apartment with her mother than she might in a busy restaurant.

Naomi was close on Emily's heels.

"I'm making a pot roast."

"Oh."

Emily turned to look at her mother. "What's the matter? You like pot roast."

"I've decided to give up eating meat."

"Since when?"

Naomi patted her nearly flat stomach. "Since I got on the scale at the health club the other morning."

"Mother, you have a fabulous figure for—" Emily stopped herself, but it was too late.

"Go on, say it. For a woman my age."

Growing old had never sat well with Naomi Bauer, but Emily knew that age had become a particularly sore point since her father had gone off and married a woman half her mother's age.

"You look fabulous for a woman of any age."

Naomi gave a half smile. "I suppose . . . a slice of pot roast wouldn't hurt."

Emily began setting the table.

"I just don't think he's all that happy," Naomi said, straightening the silverware as Emily laid each piece down.

Emily didn't have to ask whom her mother was talking about. "Wine?"

"A touch." Naomi watched her daughter uncork a bottle of Zinfandel. "I don't know if it's the new job, New York City, or . . . his marriage. Maybe some of all three."

"I got a note from Liza just last week and she says they're both terrific."

"She writes you?" The way Naomi said it, one would have thought Liza had committed one of the seven deadly sins.

"Why shouldn't she write me? We used to be roommates."

"Not for very long."

Emily gave her mother an impatient look. "She didn't steal my boyfriend away, Mother. And let's face it. If it wasn't Liza, it would have been someone else. Chris never felt about me the way I . . . felt about him."

"Men. They don't know what they feel. Above the neck."

"Mother," Emily said with a surprised laugh.

Naomi gave a dismissive wave. "I think your pot roast must be done," she said primly.

A few minutes later they sat down to eat.

Naomi cut a minuscule slice of meat and stabbed it with her fork. "Are you dating at all?"

"I go out," Emily replied vaguely.

"With a man?"

Emily sighed. She knew they were in for a round of twenty questions. Perhaps she could deflect some of them. "What about you?"

"What about me?"

"Are you going out?"

"Really, Emily."

"Really, Mother. Why shouldn't you start dating?" Emily knew the answer without needing one from her mother. Naomi didn't date for the same reason she didn't date. Because somewhere in the back of their sad, twisted minds, they kept holding out hope that the men they loved would someday return to the fold. And because they inevitably found themselves measuring every new man they met against the ones that had stolen their hearts. None ever measured up.

"I saw that young man again."

Emily looked up. "What young man?"

"I don't remember his name. You know who I mean. The one we met up in San Francisco at the—"

"David? You saw David? Where?"

"At the health club. He plays squash there. With a very attractive man. Blond, robust, a devilish smile . . ."

"Why, Mother, you sound smitten," Emily teased.

"Honestly, Emily. I was thinking that he might be someone you'd be interested in. He's a lawyer. Very successful, if the Porsche convertible he drives is any indication. And very charming."

"Did he take you for a spin?"

"Of course not. That other man—what's his name?"

"David."

"Yes, David. Well, David spotted me and stopped to say hello. I must say I was surprised he remembered who I was."

"You're unforgettable, Mother."

"Don't tease. It's not becoming."

Emily wasn't teasing. For better or worse, her mother had a way of making an indelible impression on people.

"Anyway," Naomi went on, "he introduced me to his friend. Alan Freese. And we chatted for a bit."

"Forget about Alan."

"What do you mean?"

"He's dating Cheryl."

"Cheryl from your office?"

"Don't sound so surprised. Cheryl is a terrific catch."

"I certainly think you're a lot more attractive than Cheryl. Better figure, better bone structure . . ."

"You're my mother. You have to think those things."

Naomi observed her daughter closely. "He mentioned that he saw you recently."

"Alan? Oh, at the Chinese restaurant."

"Not Alan. The other one."

"David. It's not a hard name to remember, Mother."

"You're very touchy. You seem to get irritated every time I mention his name."

"*You* don't mention his *name*. You can't even remember his name."

"*You* have no trouble remembering it."

Emily threw up her hands. "I give up. You've got me, Mother. I'm wildly, passionately in love with David Turner. He makes my temperature soar. He makes my pulse race. I've never felt so fulfilled, so ecstatic, so . . ." She slammed down her fork, her face flushed with frustration, anger, confusion—and something else; something indefinable, or at least something she refused to define. "I wish I were in love with

David. I wish he were in love with me. It would be great. It would make life so simple. For both of us."

Naomi's expression softened. "Life never is simple. For any of us. There are so many curveballs. And usually they're being thrown at you when you least expect them."

Emily smiled tenderly at her mother. "I didn't know you were a baseball aficionada."

DAVID LOOKED AROUND at the group. He'd been coming to these sessions for several weeks now. Six men, ranging from twenty-three to sixty-two, meeting with a group leader in his mid-forties every Thursday night to discuss their struggles with loss, failure, codependency, stress, and problems with intimacy. Each time David came, he asked himself what he was doing here. Oh, not that he didn't have enough of the *right* type of problems. It was just that talking about them here, with these men, being prompted by John, the group leader, didn't seem to make him feel any better or any more resolved. He couldn't help but compare how different it was for him talking to Emily. Emily...

"So, tell us more about her," Tom a thin, aesthetic-looking stockbroker in his late thirties, prodded.

David looked up, realizing Tom was addressing him. "Emily?"

All eyes turned to him. "Emily?" John inquired in that quiet-yet-insinuating tone. "I thought her name was Liza."

David flushed. "It is Liza."

"So, who's Emily?" Bill, the twenty-three-year-old college grad student asked, a gleeful smirk on his face.

"Don't tell me," Larry, the shoe salesman said with a grin, "that you're two-timing Liza."

"If he found himself a new girl," Maury, the elder statesman of the group, declared, "I say mazel tov. Congratulations. If I could find a woman who could be even half the

woman my Gert was—may she rest in peace—I'd be satis-
fied."

Grant, a bartender who characterized himself as a womanizer in search of a lost love, had another point of view. "I
don't think it works. Believe me, I've tried. Maggie was my
one great love, and no matter how many women I take to
bed, no matter how great it is, they just don't make the grade.
They're not Maggie."

"You don't understand," David said, addressing the whole
group. "Emily's not my lover. That is . . ."

"You're ambivalent?" John suggested.

"It's sort of . . . complicated."

"Did you sleep with her?" Bill asked.

David began to feel agitated. "That's not the point."

Titters and smiles all around—save from the group leader,
who observed David with a Freud-like expression.

"Go on, David," he urged, cracking his knuckles.

"Emily's in love with Liza's husband," David said quietly.

Maury shook his head and scowled. "Not good."

"You're sleeping with a woman who's doing it with the
love-of-your-life's hubby?" Grant raised his eyebrows.

"No. No, of course not. She's never slept with Chris."

"Wait," Larry broke in. "Emily's in love with Chris, but
she's never slept with him."

"What's so shocking about that?" David retorted defensively. "I've never slept—" He stopped short, but it was too
late.

Even John's eyes widened.

David glared at them all. "There's no law that says you
can't be in love without making love." He rose from his seat,
his glare deepening. "Just like there's no law that says you
can't make love without being in love."

"You're very angry," John reflected calmly.

"You're damn straight, I'm angry. I don't think any of you get the picture."

The group leader regarded him with a benign smile. "Do you think it's significant that you brought Emily's name up this evening, David?"

EMILY SANK DOWN ON HER couch after her mother left. She was emotionally exhausted from the evening. And restless.

She popped up from the couch and checked her watch, thinking she might be able to catch a late movie. Ten-fifteen. Probably too late by the time she got over to the theater.

A walk. A good, brisk walk in the fresh air. Well, not exactly *fresh*. There'd been a smog alert that morning. Still, the quality of the air was usually better at this time of night.

DAVID FELT AGITATED and at loose ends when he left the community center where the group held its meeting. Several members invited him to join them for a beer, but David begged off. He didn't think he'd be back for their next meeting. What was the point if it wasn't helping him?

When he pulled up in front of his building twenty minutes later, he stayed sitting behind the wheel, keeping the motor running. His eyes fell on the clock on the dash. Ten-fifteen.

He tapped his fingers against the steering wheel. He wasn't ready to go upstairs and call it a night. Maybe he'd take a drive, stop somewhere and have a cappuccino.

OKAY, SO SHE HAPPENED to be on his block, right by his place. She blamed it on her mother. It was her mother who'd brought David up in the conversation that evening. Not that Emily could deny that she'd been thinking about David Turner a lot these past couple of weeks. Especially when she slipped into moping over Chris. After a while, she'd find herself thinking about how nice it had been having someone she could unburden herself to. She'd find herself wanting to ring David up or get together with him, but had fought the urge. At least, until now.

She stood there on the sidewalk, locked in a silent debate. Should she stop up or not? That other evening she'd spent with him in his loft had been nice. She really did feel that he was a true soul mate. Okay, things had gotten a little dicey toward the end, but they'd come through the moment with flying colors. It was natural enough, Emily told herself, to confuse gratitude—even comfort—with desire.

She was practically at the front door of his building by this point. Was he even awake? Alone? What if he was entertaining another woman? Ignoring her flurry of disquiet, Emily told herself it would be good for David to start dating. Maybe some day, he'd wake up and realize that Liza wasn't worth his love and adoration.

DAVID'S FOOT HIT THE brakes even before his mind registered that he was practically at Emily's front door. He counted up seven floors, locating her windows. Her lights were on. She must be home. What if she wasn't alone? What if she was up there with a date? A funny feeling came over him even as he told himself he approved. One thing was clear in his mind: He honestly didn't think Chris Anders was worth Emily Bauer's devotion.

EMILY STOOD ON THE doorstep downstairs, her finger hesitating as she located the right buzzer. What was she going to say if he answered? *Hi, I just happened to be in the neighborhood?* What a pathetically transparent line. *Hi. I'm feeling a little agitated. I just spent a whole evening listening to my mother tell me that she thinks Chris looks unhappy.* She felt a bit better about that opening. It was true, for one thing. She might even ask David if he'd heard anything from Liza that led him to think there might be trouble in paradise. *Wishful thinking.*

She took a deep breath, but it was several moments before she mustered the courage to actually press the buzzer. One quick buzz, then she pulled her hand away and waited.

DAVID FOUND A PARKING space up the street. He approached Emily's building, feeling decidedly tentative. Then, once he was there, he stood outside the lobby, arms folded across his chest, trying to decide if this was such a good idea.

I'll see if she wants to go out and have a cappuccino. I won't even go up to her apartment. I'll wait down here. We can go sit in a nice, public café and chat. Completely innocent. No chance of her reading anything into that. The question was, Was there anything to read into it? He wished he knew.

There was only one way to find out. He pressed the buzzer beside her name.

"HE WASN'T IN. OR HE wasn't answering," Emily said over lunch at Antonio's the next day.

Cheryl eyed her closely. "You don't think he was up there with another woman?"

Emily attempted a nonchalant shrug. "I hope he was."

Cheryl smiled as she snapped a breadstick in two, buttering one half. "Sure, you do."

"I mean it. I think it would be good for David to date," Emily said, poking at her noodles Alfredo.

"What about what's good for the goose being good for the gander?"

"If the right man came along . . ."

"What about David?"

Emily feigned surprise. "What about David?"

"Okay, so he's no Chris Anders. I, for one, consider that a big plus."

"Please, not the rating game again."

"Okay, you tell me. What's wrong with him?"

"Nothing's wrong with him. He's very nice. He's attractive, intelligent, talented."

"So?"

"It's not as simple as that, Cheryl."

"The looming shadow of Chris and Liza," Cheryl said dramatically.

"That's part of it."

"What's the other part?"

Emily hesitated. "It's . . . complicated."

"Emily . . ."

"Enough of the David and Emily saga. Tell me about Alan."

Cheryl smiled ruefully. "He's great. Gorgeous, successful, charming, sexy."

"So?"

Cheryl shrugged. "So, I'm not counting my chickens." She twirled a few strands of fettuccine on her fork. "He used to date Liza."

"David mentioned something about that. I don't think it was anything serious."

Cheryl popped the forkful of pasta into her mouth. "She sure did get around, our little Liza."

Emily stared at her noodles, her appetite gone. "She sure did."

DAVID FOLDED THE NOTE and tucked it in his pocket as Alan arrived at their usual table at O'Shaughnessy's.

"Fan mail?" Alan asked wryly as he slipped into his seat, tucking his attaché case under his chair.

David pretended not to hear him. "You're late."

"I'm always late. Today it was Mrs. Adler. She had a change of heart. She doesn't want to divorce her husband after all. She's decided to forgive him his indiscretions. I must be going soft. I was glad to lose the case. Maybe there is such a thing as wedded bliss." He lifted up his menu, peering over it. "A letter from Liza."

David cleared his throat. "A brief note."

"How's she doing?"

"Great, I suppose."

"You suppose?"

"She says she's doing great. Maybe I'm reading between the lines, but..." He let the sentence trail and picked up his menu. "The special is Hungarian goulash."

"How's Emily doing?"

"Emily? Fine, I guess. I haven't seen her since you took off with her girlfriend the other night at the Chinese restaurant." David deliberately omitted mentioning his unsuccessful stab at seeing Emily last night, as well as his surprising feeling of disappointment.

"Aren't you going to ask me about my evening with Cheryl?"

"I wouldn't have thought Cheryl was your type."

Alan smiled crookedly. "That's how much you know."

"She's nothing like Liza."

"That's the best thing about Cheryl." Alan's smile deepened. "The same can be said about Emily. I thought Emily was terrific."

"Maybe you'd like her phone number."

"Maybe. If things don't work out with Cheryl."

David picked up his menu and stared at it. "Fine."

Alan smiled. "I think I'll have the goulash."

"Fine."

WHEN EMILY GOT HOME from work that night, she looked at the flowers wilting in her vase and felt a profound sense of loneliness. Her eyes strayed to the telephone, then back to the flowers, which seemed to be drooping more and more with each second. She glanced back to the phone.

"This is ridiculous," she announced to her empty apartment. "Why shouldn't I call him? There's no crime in wanting to talk to him."

Sucking in a deep breath, she walked resolutely over to the phone and dialed David's number quickly, before she lost her nerve. She got his answering machine and hung up. Less than a minute later her phone rang. She was sure it was her mother and decided to let her machine pick up the message.

"Hi, Emily, it's me. David. David Turner. I was just—"

"David?"

"Emily?"

"I just tried you."

"You did?"

Emily thought he sounded pleased.

"I heard the phone ringing as I was opening the door. You didn't leave a message."

"No. I'm lousy at messages. I stammer and repeat myself and sound like a total idiot."

"No, you don't."

"How do you know?"

"Because even if you did sound like a total idiot, I'd know better."

"That's a nice thing to say."

"Emily, what do you say we start over again?"

"Start over?"

"As friends."

"Friends?"

"Why not?"

"Well . . ."

"I know. It would be a novelty. The usual route is the other way around." He hesitated. "There is another way to look at it."

"What's that?"

"Most couples who start as friends are always wondering what it would be like to be lovers."

Emily smiled. "And we already know that."

"Right."

"And we know . . . it wouldn't work."

"Right." Was there a slight pause before David answered in the affirmative?

"I don't know, David. Could we really put that night behind us? Enough for us to . . . be friends?"

"Neither of us were ourselves that night."

"That's true."

"Not that you weren't . . ."

"Oh, you were, too."

They chuckled.

"The next morning, though . . ."

"I don't know about you," Emily admitted, "but I was a wreck. I was mortified."

"I felt like a complete heel," David confessed. "I took advantage—"

"No, I was the one—"

"Can I tell you the truth, Emily?"

"Of course you can, David."

"I couldn't wait to get away that morning."

"I couldn't wait for you to leave. I only made you breakfast because I deluded myself into believing it made what had happened between us the night before seem less tawdry. I was wrong. Breakfast was torture. I couldn't even look you in the eye. All I really wanted to do was hide under the covers until you were gone. I was trying to be so . . ."

"So was I."

They both laughed. They both felt a lot better. Maybe this was going to be the start of a beautiful friendship.

6

EMILY WAS FINISHING up an editorial article for the next edition of *Chic* when Cheryl popped her head in her office. "Want to go to a movie tonight?"

Emily looked up from her monitor. "Where's Alan?"

"We both agreed we should take this thing nice and slow. That way we won't burn out too fast."

Emily nodded. "Makes sense."

"What do you say? Want to spend a couple of hours in the dark with Tom Cruise or Mel Gibson?"

"David Turner."

Cheryl stepped into Emily's office and shut the door. "You're spending a couple of hours in the dark with David Turner tonight?" A slow smile played on Cheryl's lips. "This is getting to be a habit."

"We're going to a jazz concert."

"Oh."

"We both like jazz."

"Nice."

"We were both planning to go to the concert separately. So we decided we might as well go together."

"Mmm."

"He's a friend," Emily said firmly. "We're friends. Nothing more."

"Friends. Great."

Emily was determined to put a stop to Cheryl's romantic ruminations about her and David. "He has a date tomorrow night. With one of his new models. She's very beautiful.

Brunette. High cheekbones. And tall. Very tall. Adrienne. I was the one who encouraged him to ask her out."

Cheryl smiled sweetly. "What are friends for?"

"Exactly."

"What about you?"

Emily had started to proof her copy. She looked up from her monitor, her expression blank. "What about me?"

"Any hot dates on the horizon for you?"

Emily sat up a little straighter in her swivel chair. "I'm keeping my eyes open."

"Alan has a very attractive law partner. More John Wayne than Jimmy Stewart, but still . . ."

Emily threw an eraser at her friend.

Cheryl ducked. "He even rides horses."

"I hate horses."

"Chris rode horses, didn't he?"

Emily's expression sobered, her gaze dropping to the photo of the celebrity sportscaster that she still kept on her desk. "I think my mother was right about Chris. He doesn't look good. I mean, he looks good. He always looks good. It's just that I think he looks a little frayed around the edges."

"He's in town again?"

"No, I've only seen him on television. Even on the screen you could see that twinkle in his eye is missing. There are lines at the corners of his mouth that were never there before. Stress lines. I'm sure his fans don't notice. I don't even know if Liza notices."

"The question is, why are you noticing?"

"You already know the answer."

"Emily, let me fix you up with Neal Rickman. How about next Saturday night?"

"Who's Neal Rickman?"

"Alan's law partner."

"Can't."

"Why can't you?"

"I already have a date. That is," she quickly amended, "David's invited me to fly with him up to Sacramento for the weekend."

There was that smile again. "Oh. A weekend."

"He booked separate rooms. And they're not connected."

"Why Sacramento?"

"There's going to be a big demonstration in front of the State House opposing Proposition 11."

"What's Proposition 11?"

Emily shrugged. "I'm not really sure. Something to do with a tax hike on real estate. David wants to take some photos—"

"Fashion photos? At a demonstration?"

"No. Just photos. I've been encouraging David to get a portfolio together. Did you know he's an incredible photojournalist? He only went into fashion work because of Liza."

"A photojournalist. Isn't that fascinating?"

"He happens to be exceptionally good."

"I don't doubt it for an instant."

Emily swung around in her chair and looked Cheryl straight in the eye. "Haven't you ever simply liked someone as a friend?"

Cheryl grinned. "I like you."

"A man."

"A man friend?"

"Yes," Emily said. "A man with whom you have no messy romantic entanglements, no seductive game playing, no jealousy, no—"

"No," Cheryl said succinctly.

"Then I guess you can't understand that David and I can care about each other, admire each other, enjoy each other's company, and not be interested in . . ."

"Yes?" Cheryl asked with an impish smile.

"In anything romantic," Emily finished firmly. "In fact, we're both convinced romance would spoil a lovely friendship." A lovely friendship that had started off in bed! That was behind them. Forgotten. A thing of the past. They were beginning all over again. And doing a good job of it. Weren't they?

"Personally," Cheryl said, "I'm the type that likes to mix my peas and carrots."

"What does that mean?"

"I like having a friend and lover all rolled into one."

Emily smiled wistfully. "I'm off carrots. They don't seem to agree with my digestion."

Cheryl started for the door. "When are you and David going off for your tryst?"

"Saturday morning. And it isn't a tryst."

"Okay, keep Friday night open."

"Open for what?"

"Neal Rickman."

"Cheryl . . ."

"Don't think of him as a carrot. Think of him as . . . a turnip. Similar veggie but with its own distinctive qualities."

AFTER THE JAZZ CONCERT, Emily and David stopped at a night spot in Malibu. They were sitting on the terrace overlooking the ocean, nursing their margaritas. Once again they were engrossed in their usual topic of conversation—probing the feelings they had for their "first" loves; trying to understand why they were unable to let go; what it was about Liza and Chris that had held them in the grip of unrequited love for so long. These discussions had become something of a compulsion. Or, possibly, a way to avoid talking too much about the relationship that was developing between the two of them.

"The first thing? Gosh, it's so long ago I don't know if I re-member," Emily was saying. "What about you? What was the first thing you noticed about Liza?"

David didn't hesitate. "Her hair. Short hair was in for girls in my school back then, but Liza's hair was halfway down her back. She wore it loose. Never in those dumb braids."

"I wore my hair in dumb braids back in elementary school," Emily said with a sigh.

David was immediately contrite. "I didn't mean *dumb*."

Emily gave him a no-nonsense look. "Yes, you did. If it makes you feel any better, I used to have a running battle with my mother about those braids. She said it was either the braids or cut my hair. I finally cut my hair in the fourth grade. I looked like Little Orphan Annie. Even the braids were bet-ter."

"I used to have a crew cut. All the cool guys in school had crew cuts."

"You were one of the cool guys?"

David wasn't hurt by the note of surprise in her voice. "Hardly. To be cool, you had to have more than a certain hairstyle. You had to be a jock. I had the distinction of being the only kid on my Little League team that never got a base hit for an entire season. The only time I ever got on base was when Lyle Ingram pitched. He used to walk everyone."

"I was very uncoordinated as a kid," Emily confided. "I was always one of the last ones picked in gym when we had to choose up sides for volleyball or basketball. I tried hard, but I just didn't have it in me. And there was Chris, star ath-lete—"

She stopped and smiled. "I know what it was that first at-tracted me to Chris—his legs. The first time I saw him, he was running across the school field in his gym shorts, playing soccer. He was only ten years old, but he already had mus-cles. Real muscles. I remember this group of girls standing near me and they were all giggling and ogling him, whispering to each other, making little swooning sounds whenever he kicked the ball. I stood there, mesmerized by him. And then . . ."

"Yes?" David asked.

"Oh, he took his shirt off. And he was . . . so tan. He had this fine golden body. And golden hair. He was like some kid Greek god or something." Emily's face was flushed as she took a sip of her drink.

"Liza had the same effect on me," David said with a smile. "Every time I saw her I'd find myself staring at her. I couldn't help it. She was so beautiful, so . . . perfect. I used to try to get up the nerve to talk to her, but whenever I had the opportunity, I'd break out in a sweat and get so tongue-tied I'd come off sounding like an even bigger jerk than I was."

"You weren't a jerk. You just never quite fit in. I know that feeling. All through elementary school and then junior high, I was out of it. I wore glasses, I went from braces to retainers, my hair was too frizzy. Let's just say I wasn't about to be crowned Miss Adlai Stevenson Junior High. When I got to high school, my mother finally agreed to let me get contact lenses, my teeth were nice and straight, and my hair stopped frizzing. I even lost fifteen pounds." Emily rested her elbows on the table and propped her chin in her palms. "Did Chris notice the transformation?"

"No?"

"No. Sure, I looked a lot better, but there were all these other girls who also looked better. And they'd started out looking pretty damn good in the first place. I always felt like I was playing catch-up."

"Liza and I got to be friends in high school. I think it was because I was the only male student at Edgemont High that didn't hit on her." David grinned. "Not that I didn't want to. I just didn't have the courage. Besides, I knew my competition and I was realistic enough to know I was out of the running."

"Chris and I got to be friends in high school, but if I'm going to be honest with myself I have to admit it was more my doing than Chris's. I worked hard at getting him to see me as someone he could count on in a pinch, someone he could turn to, someone he could rely on."

"Did it work?"

Emily nodded. "Yeah. I became Good Old Em, steadfast and true. Chris would even drop over to my house sometimes—if he needed help with a paper or wanted to talk about some girl he was dating. You could bet he never stopped by on a Saturday night."

"Did you go out with other guys?" David asked.

"Yes, but mostly to try to make Chris jealous. Or at least to get him to notice that other boys were interested. It didn't work. He was too caught up in his own romantic conquests. We even doubled once. It was awful." She finished off her drink.

"Do you want another one?"

"No, thanks. It's getting late. We probably should get going."

"It was a good concert, wasn't it?"

"Terrific. I love the Modern Jazz Quartet."

"I'm glad we went together."

Emily smiled. "So am I. I never thought I'd say this, but I feel really comfortable with you, David. You're my first male friend."

"What about Chris?"

"That was different. I never allowed myself to be myself around Chris. I tried to be alluring, witty, mysterious. Unfortunately, I didn't know how to be any of those things. I kept trying anyway, forever angling to win him over, get him to love me. I could never be open with him. I could never share my real feelings."

"I know," David said softly. "It was the same for me and Liza. I was always trying to be someone else. The kind of guy I thought she'd want. I was always posing, always playing a role. Playing it badly."

"Will you do that with Adrienne? Play a role?"

"Adrienne?" For a minute David forgot all about the model he had a date with the following night. "Oh, Adrienne." David frowned. "I don't know if this date is such a good idea."

"Of course, it's a good idea," Emily said firmly. "We both agreed it was totally idiotic for us to spend the rest of our lives pining away over Chris and Liza."

"We both agreed, but I'm the one going out."

Emily pressed her lips together. "So am I."

David didn't conceal his look of surprise. "You are? You didn't tell me."

"It just came up today. I'm not certain—"

"Who?"

"Oh, it's really Cheryl's doing. She's determined to fix me up."

"With who?" David persisted.

"Alan's law partner."

"Neal Rickman?"

Emily scrutinized David's expression. Was that a frown? Did he disapprove? "Yes. Do you know him?"

David studied the remnants of his margarita as if he were a fortune-teller reading tea leaves. "Just casually." His tone was deliberately bland.

Emily reached across the table and gripped David's sleeve. "Hey, friend. Be straight with me. You don't like him, do you?"

David met her gaze. "No. I think he's too slick, too sure of himself, too self-centered." He had to restrain himself from saying that Neal Rickman reminded him a lot of Chris Anders.

He didn't have to say it. Emily knew it was what he was thinking. And she didn't like it. "It's not a crime to be self-confident. I happen to admire men who go after what they want."

"Well, then, I imagine you and Neal will hit it off nicely," David said tightly, presuming that Emily was taking a dig at him for not having pursued his dreams.

"We might at that," Emily replied crisply, feeling hurt and betrayed by David's roundabout attack on Chris.

There was a long silence. Then their anger began to ebb, both of them acknowledging that they'd overreacted. Nerves? Tentative smiles played on their lips.

"I'm sorry," David said quietly. "Maybe I'm jealous of men like Neal." He hesitated. "Men like Chris."

Emily was touched by David's honesty. "I know Chris comes across as self-satisfied, but you've got to admit he's great at what he does. And he loves it."

David's irritation faded, his expression thoughtful. "What you just said about admiring men who go after what they want . . ." He paused, his gaze drifting out toward the darkened sea. "I've been lying to myself for years telling myself I'm happy being a fashion photographer. It doesn't even have anything to do with whether or not I'm good at it. The work does nothing for my soul. If I could get some paper or magazine interested in my news photos, I'd give up fashion work in a snap. I know I'd feel damn good about myself as a photojournalist."

"You'd have every reason to feel good. I'd feel good, too. I'd like to see you happy."

"I'd like to see you happy, too, Emily. What about you taking the plunge?"

"The plunge?"

"Why not try to get a job at the kind of magazine you really want to work at?"

"It's not so bad at *Chic*. There is a kind of glamour—" She stopped. "Who am I kidding? I took a job at a fashion magazine to impress Chris. I thought if I was surrounded by all that glamour, some of it would wear off." She sighed.

"Okay, maybe we can't get everything we want, Emily," David said, his features taking on a sharp intensity. "But why not get what we can?"

"Why not?" she murmured.

His hand reached across the table. "Shall we shake on it?"

Emily hesitated. She wasn't quite sure what they were shaking on. Yet, when her hand made contact with his, she wasn't all that sure that it mattered at all.

Their eyes locked as their grip tightened. They both let go quickly. Another silence ensued, this one laced with an altogether different type of tension.

A short while later, as David pulled up in front of Emily's apartment, she moved impulsively toward him and brushed her lips against his cheek, determined to reestablish their platonic bond of friendship.

"Have a nice time tomorrow night," she said brightly, disturbed that her tone sounded a bit artificial.

David gave her a blank look.

"With Adrienne."

"Oh. Right. I will," he said so solemnly, he might have been taking his date to a wake.

Emily was halfway out of the car when David said, "Neal's a nice enough guy once you get to know him. I hope the two of you hit it off."

They smiled at each other, but the smiles were forced. And they both knew it.

DAVID WAS NERVOUSLY watching the clock over the check-in counter as he paced the terminal. The flight for Sacramento left in twenty minutes. Emily was already ten minutes late. That wasn't like her. She was always prompt. Could she have overslept?

David frowned. She'd gone out with Neal Rickman last night. He'd probably brought her home late—if he'd brought her home at all....

David's pacing picked up speed. *Okay, so what if they did sleep together? Why should it bother me?* He stopped, thinking he'd spotted her. He was wrong.

All right, it bothers me. Emily's my friend. I care about her. I don't think Neal's the right kind of guy for her. Neal's a womanizer. Emily's bound to get hurt. She doesn't deserve that.

Who are you kidding? You're jealous. You don't like the idea of Emily going to bed with another guy. The thought of some other man kissing her, caressing her, being tantalized by her fragrance is gnawing at you. You're attracted to her. You're not so sure you want your relationship to be strictly platonic. Admit it.

That's crazy. I'm not jealous. I'm concerned. Emily's my friend and I like it that way. I'm not ready for another roller-coaster ride. I'm just beginning to get over Liza—or I'm trying to convince myself I am. I'm going to put all my energy into getting going as a photojournalist. Having a romantic entanglement would complicate things. Especially with Emily. Besides, she's still in love with Chris.

Or had she switched her affections to Neal Rickman? It was possible. Neal and Chris had enough in common.

David jumped as he felt a hand on his shoulder. His face was flushed as he spun around to find Emily standing there.

She felt him surveying her purposefully, as if inspecting her for some sign of malfunction.

"I should have had you pick me up after all," she said breathlessly. "My car got a flat tire on the freeway. What a nightmare. A cabbie stopped and helped me or I never would have gotten here."

"Are you okay? Do you still want to go?"

"Are you kidding? I need this trip. I need to get away from L.A. My mother found out I had an actual date last night and she was on the phone the first thing this morning, giving me the third degree. I know it's nuts, but she's got it in her head that Chris and Liza are going to split up one of these days and that I shouldn't rush into another relationship just in case Chris finally sees the light."

"How did the date with Neal go?"

Emily took his arm. "I'll tell you on the plane. And you have to tell me all about your night on the town with Adrienne," she added in a light tone that belied her true feelings. It had bothered her more than she cared to admit that she hadn't heard from David since his date. Had things gone better than he'd expected? Better than she'd expected? Or wanted?

THEY HAD JUST BARELY settled into their seats when David turned to Emily, who was snapping her seat belt.

"Did you have a good time?"

Emily shot David a look. "Do you know that Neal's a genius?"

"A genius?"

"Yes," she said dramatically. "He told me so himself. Several times. It was like listening to the Elizabeth Barrett Browning poem. Only in Neal's version it was, 'How do I love *me*? Let me count the ways.' Which he did. Ad infinitum. And ad nauseam."

A big smile lit up David's face. "That bad?"

"You don't have to look so happy. I had a miserable time. I did get something out of it, though."

"What's that?"

"I'm not even going to attempt dating for a while. It's not just that Neal was so pompous and boring and that his ego is so inflated I was sorely tempted to jab him with a pin and watch him pop. I realized even before he arrived I wasn't ready. Anyway, what you said the other night about my job at *Chic* not being for me was right on the mark. I'm going to spend the next few months concentrating on making changes in my career, trying to achieve a sense of accomplishment and satisfaction in my work. I don't have space for a man in my life right now."

"I see," David said softly.

Emily's hand shot out and she gripped his arm. "I didn't mean you."

David grinned. "I don't know how I should take that."

Emily squeezed his arm. "You know what I mean."

"You mean that the whole time you were out with Neal, all you did was think about Chris."

Emily nodded, even though his assessment wasn't completely true. A couple of times last night, she'd also found herself thinking about David. She let go of his arm.

"Letting go isn't easy," he murmured.

"How was your date with Adrienne?"

David grinned. "My only regret is that I didn't give her Neal's number. I think they'd be a perfect match. If they could fit their two oversize egos into one car."

"That bad?"

"Let's say she has three main interests in life. Herself, herself, and herself."

They laughed and settled back into their seats, feeling relaxed for the first time that morning.

A few minutes after the plane was airborne, David turned to her. "What I said before—about letting go not being easy?"

"Yes?"

"I think I'm beginning to get a better perspective on my feelings about Liza."

Emily's expression was somewhat suspect. "I'm all ears."

"I won't deny that when I think about her—and I suppose I still do think about her a fair amount—I feel this sort of ache in my heart for what I wanted to happen between us...." He paused, before adding wistfully, "and what never would have happened, even if Chris hadn't come along. There would have been another Chris."

Emily nodded. She was thinking the same about her and Chris. If not Liza, then another woman very much like Liza would have stolen Chris's heart.

"I'm making progress, though. I'm beginning to come to terms with the reality," David said earnestly. "I think that's very important. Accepting the reality. Not clinging to fantasy. Getting on with my life."

"Not every woman is like Adrienne," Emily said quietly. "If you keep going out you'll find someone...."

David smiled disarmingly. "I guess I'm not ready to find someone. I feel the same way you do about dating at this point. I need some time to regroup." He took hold of her hand. "It's definitely easier doing that with you, Emily. I can relax around you, be myself. Our friendship means a lot to me."

Emily felt her eyes mist over. "It means a lot to me, too, David." Her expression became serious. "I just hope nothing ever happens to spoil it." Her voice held a tentative note. She couldn't stop herself from wondering if it was possible to have a love affair with a friend. Even as that thought entered her mind, she knew she was treading on dangerous ground. Besides, the next time she went to bed with a man, she wanted it to be with someone who wasn't wrapped up in another woman. And for all of David's lip service about getting over Liza, Emily was dubious.

David could feel the tremor in her hand. Or was it his? "Nothing will ever happen to spoil our friendship, Emily." His voice lacked conviction. And his heart was pumping double time. Emily may have been his friend, but she was also a beautiful, desirable woman in her own special way. Suddenly, at an altitude of seven thousand feet, David was consumed with a wave of carnal lust. The scent of her perfume wafted over him, alluring, tantalizing, intoxicating.

"David, what's wrong?"

He felt sick with guilt. Here Emily was, filled with trust and hope over their friendship, and here he was, letting his mind drift into erotic fantasy. He was also furious with himself for once again being drawn to a woman who was in love with another man. He knew that Emily had no more gotten over Chris than he had gotten over Liza. At least he was trying. Was Emily?

David struggled for a benign expression. "Wrong?"

Emily looked down at their entwined hands—David's grip so tight, the blood was draining from her fingers. He smiled sheepishly and released his hold. "Sorry."

"I thought you liked to fly."

"I do. I guess I was just thinking—"

"About Liza?"

David didn't respond.

Emily patted his arm. "It's okay, David. You can't expect yourself to accept the reality, as you put it, in one fell swoop."

THINGS WERE ALREADY heating up in front of the State House by the time Emily and David arrived. A rabble-rouser was at the microphone working a large portion of the crowd into a frenzy. Activists on both sides of the issue had shown up to express their opinions. There was a lot of pushing and shoving going on. A police contingent was moving in to try to keep the peace.

Emily nudged David, pointing to a fight that had broken out between two middle-aged men while two women stood by cheering their respective mates on.

David snapped the shot, then turned to Emily. "I think you ought to go back to the hotel and wait for me. Things could get out of control here and I don't want you to get hurt."

"I won't get hurt. Remember, I took a course in self-defense," Emily countered with an air of self-assurance. "Besides, this could be a great opportunity for me, too."

"How's that?"

She dug in her purse for a notepad and a pen. "I think I'll do a little freelance reporting. Go around and get some on-the-spot interviews and write them up. I could send it around with my résumé."

"Emily, if something happened to you here, I'd never forgive myself."

"I'll be fine, David. Don't worry about me."

"I come from a long line of worriers. It's in my blood. I'm good at it."

Emily smiled, then ducked into the crowd. Within seconds David had lost sight of her.

As he made his own way through the agitated crowd, snapping photos, David wasn't able to pay full attention to the action. He was worried about Emily. Several brawls had broken out. A group of young people who didn't even seem to know what the demonstration was about had joined in and the scene was starting to get ugly. The police were rounding up troublemakers and carting them into cruisers.

David began searching in earnest for Emily. He was angry with himself. They should have picked a meeting spot away from the fracas. He shouldn't have let her go off like she had in the first place. With the tensions and skirmishes escalating at the rate they were, a course in self-defense wasn't going to keep Emily out of harm's way.

A bottle whizzed right by David's head, crashing to the ground a few feet in front of him. Glass shattered, one of the shards flying up and catching him in the arm, drawing blood. Ignoring the superficial gash, David's only concern was finding Emily and getting her out of there.

"Hey, buddy, get a picture of this," a bruiser of a man shouted in David's direction just as he was about to sock a demonstrator in the jaw.

A woman standing behind the instigator swung her pocketbook at him, cuffing his ear. "Pick on someone your own size," she snapped.

David's mouth dropped open even before he got a good look at the woman. He'd recognized her voice. "Emily..."

Before David got another word out or was able to get another step closer, the man Emily had attacked swung around and was about to land his fist in her face.

Emily ducked in the nick of time, even managing a jab into the man's gut. It was an ineffectual blow, she saw a moment later as the man made a grab for her.

Shoving his camera bag over his shoulder, David darted to Emily's defense.

"Let go of her!" he demanded, his hand clamping down hard on the brawny man's shoulder.

The man turned to David, a slow, grim smile spreading across his beefy face. "You want to make me?" he taunted in a low, gruff voice.

Emily's breath caught. As relieved as she was that David had come to her rescue, she was terrified that this bruiser would make mincemeat of him. She tried to intercede, at the same time attempting to struggle out of the man's grasp. "Can't we all just...?"

"If that's the way you want it," David hissed, eyeballing the bruiser. They may have been close to the same height, but David's opponent had a good thirty pounds on him. And it was all muscle.

Emily's face registered panic. "David . . ." There was fear and urgency in her voice.

"Whatcha gonna do, David?" the bruiser taunted.

David not only came from a long line of worriers, but from a long line of firm believers in talking rather than fighting their way out of predicaments. This was one predicament David knew he wasn't going to get out of by talking.

A small group had gathered around them, though no one was interested in coming to either side's aid. If anything, they were ready to watch a good fight. David didn't know how good it was going to be, but he was certain it would be quick.

The bruiser's taunting smile was replaced by a hard grimace. David took a deep breath, clenched his teeth and curled his hand into a tight fist. As he got ready to swing, Emily managed to distract the bruiser by kicking him hard in the shin.

David's fist landed smack on the guy's jaw, catching him completely off guard. For an instant, David was afraid his blow had made little impact. The man stood there, stunned, rigid. Then he swayed toward David, reaching for him, catching hold of the strap of his camera bag. The strap dug into David's shoulder as the injured man attempted to keep his balance. David stepped back. As the man started to sag to the ground, the strap slipped off David's shoulder.

The bag full of expensive camera equipment hit the pavement a second or two after the man. David groaned, imagining the damage he'd find when he opened the bag. Meanwhile, the demonstrators who had witnessed David "slay Goliath" cheered.

"David, your camera!" Emily gasped, as he bent down to retrieve the canvas case. Then she saw the blood oozing from the cut in his arm. "Oh, no! You're bleeding."

"It's nothing," he said hurriedly, grabbing the strap of his camera bag with one hand, Emily's arm with the other. He was more than eager to get away from there before the fallen man got back to his feet.

Emily, who was feeling horribly guilty, saw the man start to rise and she quickly applied one of her self-defense moves, much to the crowd's delight. Unfortunately, the two policemen who'd arrived on the scene were far from gleeful. As they moved into squelch the fracas, the crowd quickly dispersed.

Neither Emily or David could believe it when the officers grabbed them, seeing them as the instigators—a fact that the bruiser, who was still sitting on the pavement rubbing his jaw, quickly confirmed.

"It's a lie," Emily said indignantly. "He was the one—"

"Please, officer, I can explain," David interrupted, trying his best to stay calm. "My girlfriend and I were here to cover the demonstration. We're journalists. This troublemaker started to attack Emily—"

"I'm not the troublemaker. I was just standing here—"

"Well, actually," Emily cut in, eager to clarify the situation, "he was about to attack someone else and I told him he ought to pick on someone his own size and he—"

"She clobbered me over the head with her pocketbook," the bruiser whined. "Caught me hard, right in the ear. Now I'm hearing this ringing sound."

"Liar," Emily hissed, then turned back to the policemen. "Then he grabbed me...."

The younger officer gave her a narrow look. "Which one?"

"That one, of course," Emily said impatiently, pointing her finger at the bruiser.

"And I warned him to take his hands off her," David piped in.

Emily smiled timorously at David. "You were a regular knight in shining armor."

David smiled back, feeling a flash of macho pride, temporarily forgetting his certain-to-be-broken camera, the gash on his arm, his sore fist, even the skeptical policemen.

"I want to issue a complaint. Against both of them," the bruiser demanded, making a big show of struggling to his feet. "A broken jaw, a busted eardrum—"

"Oh, give it a rest," Emily snapped. She turned to the two cops. "We're the ones who want to press charges...."

"Emily," David said with a little shake of his head. "Look, officers, all we were doing was our job...."

"And just what newspaper do you two work for?" one of the policemen asked, flipping open a pad.

"It's not a newspaper. It's a ... magazine," Emily said, her voice sounding a little wilted. She looked over at David, knowing that he was thinking the same thing she was thinking. That it wasn't going to win them any points with the Sacramento police when they found out that she worked for *Chic* and that David was a free-lance fashion photographer. How were they going to explain to these cops, whose patience was wearing thin, that this was the start of their venturing into new, more meaningful careers?

THREE HOURS AND FOUR hundred dollars later, Emily and David stepped out of the police station, dirty, disheveled and exhausted.

Emily looked over at David's bandaged cut. "Do you want to have a doctor look at your arm?"

"No."

"You might need stitches."

"I don't," he said tersely, hoisting the strap of his camera bag higher up on his shoulder.

"I'm so sorry about your camera, David," Emily said as they started down the concrete steps.

"Maybe I can salvage the roll, anyway," he said wearily.

Emily came to a stop a few steps from the sidewalk. "It's my fault. Go on and say it."

David kept walking. "It's not your fault, Emily."

"You're sorry you took me."

"I'm not sorry. I guess I simply don't understand why you . . . got involved."

She hurried down the steps after him. "I just saw red when that ape grabbed that poor guy who was half his size."

David shot her a look. "And you weren't less than half his size?"

"You *are* mad. You blame me. You think if I—"

"Don't tell me what I think, Emily."

"Well, you don't have to snap at me."

"I wasn't snapping. I am not in the habit of snapping at people."

They reached the curb. David's features were grim as he hailed a cab. He didn't know why he was in such a dark mood now that it was all over.

A cab pulled up. Emily grabbed the door handle, deciding not to wait to see if David was going to open the door for her.

David slid in beside her. "The Marion Hotel, please," he said to the cabbie. He said nothing to the woman sitting beside him.

IT WASN'T UNTIL EMILY was up in the bathroom of her hotel room, under the soothing hot shower, that it struck her that when David was having his "discussion" with the two policemen, he had called her his girlfriend. *My girlfriend and I were here to cover the demonstration. My girlfriend and I . . .*

Why had he called her his girlfriend? Did he think the policemen would be more sympathetic if they thought they were more than friends? Was it merely a slip of the tongue? Were his feelings for her changing? Were hers for him?

She sighed as she began to massage a capful of shampoo into her hair. David really had been terrific, coming to her aid the way he had. And then in the police cruiser and even down at the police station, he'd been so protective and solicitous of her. Not to mention talking the desk sergeant into letting them off with only a fine.

Once they were released though, David had been in such a foul mood. Not that she could blame him. He was out four hundred bucks, even though she'd offered to pay the fine or split it with him. His camera and several lenses had been ruined. He had a gash on his arm, and his hand was swollen. And it was all her fault. She should have known better than to have started something with an obvious bully.

Still, she had gotten some wonderful interviews for the article that she planned to write. Hopefully the article would demonstrate her talent as a journalist. If David could salvage the roll of film he'd snapped at the demonstration, the pictures would add weight to his portfolio. Wouldn't it be something if they both ended up working at news magazines?

She smiled, ignoring the suds dripping down her face. Coming to Sacramento with David had been a real eye-opener. She'd gotten to see a whole new side to her "friend" that afternoon—a side of him that was tough, chivalrous, brave, even a little reckless. And altogether appealing.

As she rinsed out her hair, she realized that, whatever his reason, she'd liked hearing him refer to her as his girlfriend. More than liked it. It gave her a little thrill.

The thrill was quickly followed by a panic attack.

7

THEY DIDN'T GET TOGETHER until that evening, downstairs in
the hotel dining room. As they sat across from each other at
the white linen-covered table, their faces lit by candlelight,
both were going out of their way to be inordinately polite.

"Are you sure the steak isn't too rare?" David asked solic-
itously.

"No. It's fine," Emily assured him primly, carefully trim-
ming off a piece of fat. "How's your trout?"

"Excellent." He reached for the wine bottle. "Some more?"

"Just half a glass, thank you."

He poured precisely that amount.

She lifted the breadbasket. "The buns are very good."

A smile flickered on his lips, but only for an instant. "No,
thanks."

She set the basket down and tried to concentrate on her
steak. She had no appetite. She felt as though she were in
mourning for the easy camaraderie and rapport she and David had worked so hard to achieve, and which now seemed
to have been eradicated because of some dumb demonstration.

No. It wasn't really the demonstration. It was the feelings
that had been churned up because of that incident and their
subsequent arrest. It was her seeing David in a whole new
light; recognizing that he was not only an attractive and appealing man, but that he was attractive and appealing to her.
It was being stirred by that look of macho pride on his face
when he'd knocked her would-be assailant out. It was the

way her heart sped up when he'd put his arm around her in the police cruiser. It had really begun before their arrival in Sacramento, back at LAX when she'd felt a wave of relief that David's date with Adrienne had gone as badly as hers had with Neal.

She glanced over at David now. He looked very handsome in an off-white linen sport jacket over dark trousers and a hunter-green shirt that echoed his green eyes. The tight, drawn look that she'd seen on his face when they left the precinct was gone, but it had been replaced by an equally disturbing blandness. Was she now going to lose him even as a friend?

He caught her observing him. "Are you sure there isn't a problem with the steak?"

She shook her head. "I'm just not very hungry."

David looked down at his barely touched trout. "Neither am I." He set his fork down.

"I suppose we should be grateful we're not dining on bread and water tonight," she said, trying for levity.

She did manage to coax a small smile from David. "That's the first time I've ever been arrested. Being a photojournalist is a lot riskier than snapping pictures of models."

"Are you having second thoughts?" She wasn't only referring to his potential career switch.

David lifted his napkin from his lap and put it down on the table. "I developed those pictures I got today. Over at a photography studio down the street."

Her breath held. "Did they . . . come out okay?"

It was his first real smile that evening. Emily had never imagined a mere smile could have such an exhilarating effect on her.

"Come up to my room and see for yourself."

Emily accepted without hesitation.

Alone in the elevator, they found themselves standing close together. Aware of each other's scent. Her perfume. His after-shave.

As they passed the second floor David apologized for his surly mood after they left the police station. "I was blaming myself, but I took it out on you."

"If I'd minded my own business . . ."

"It's because you care. That's a very fine quality. You have a lot of fine qualities, Emily," he said softly.

"So do you, David." Her voice was almost a whisper, her gaze straying from his face to his lanky body; a body she'd once caressed, stroked, explored, but not one she'd fully appreciated. She doubted she would make that same mistake twice. . . .

David tentatively extended his hand. "Friends?"

She forced a bright smile as she took his hand. "Friends." Neither of them wanted to let go.

FRIENDSHIP WASN'T WHAT was on either of their minds as they stepped into David's hotel room. The room was dimly lit by a lamp on an end table beside his bed. He didn't reach for the light switch. As he closed the door their gazes connected and held for several seconds too long to pretend camaraderie.

Nervously, Emily turned her head away. It wasn't that she was oblivious to the potent hint behind David's lingering glance. Any more than she thought he was oblivious to hers. They were both getting across the message of mutual desire. The problem was, that message was tangled up with so many others.

Why does he want me? Emily thought. *Is he settling? In the back of his mind, will he always be comparing me to Liza? How much does he really care? How much can he care and still carry a torch for her?*

Similar questions were tormenting David about Emily and her feelings for Chris. He felt like he was competing with a phantom.

Emily was compelled to break the silence. "The pictures."

David looked blankly at Emily.

"The ones you developed," she reminded him.

They were on the bedside table beneath the lamp. Emily sat primly on the edge of the bed and went through them very slowly. "They're . . . great."

David sat down beside her, leaving only inches between them. "Do you really think so?"

"I do." She glanced at him. "Honestly."

Again their gazes lingered. Then his dropped to her full, inviting breasts, camouflaged by the soft, filmy silk of her lilac blouse. Slowly, he made his way back to her face, zeroing in on her rose-shaded lips. "Emily, honesty is very important. I've always valued that in our relationship."

"So have I," she replied earnestly. "If we can't be honest with each other at this point, who can we—"

"Emily, I want to kiss you." An enticing smile played on his lips. "Honestly."

"David . . ."

He didn't wait to hear any more, and his mouth moved over hers, drowning out whatever she meant to say.

She meant to say yes.

When Emily felt the press of his mouth on hers, her lips parted invitingly, eagerly. Her hands came up and cupped his face. The photos fluttered to the carpet. Neither of them noticed.

David's fingers slipped through Emily's hair, drawing the strands away from her face. Her lovely face. Her warm brown eyes. Her sweetly upturned nose. Her soft, full, sensual lips.

His arms moved around her waist and he drew her closer. Her breasts flattening against his chest, one of her legs finding its way over his. They fell back on the bed, continuing to kiss greedily.

Does it really have to be love? both of them were thinking. Wouldn't a lot of "like" do? *Yes, yes, yes,* they told themselves as they frantically helped each other out of their clothes, kissing all the while.

For a few brief moments, Liza flitted through David's mind. Liza and Emily were so different—in looks, style, personality. The comparisons, however, did not find Emily wanting. Quite the contrary.

A vision of Chris Anders also rose in David's mind, a Greek godlike face smiling mockingly down at him. Liza. Emily. Both Chris's women!

He drew confidence from reminding himself that Emily was in *his* arms; her fine, soft, naked body was pressed against *his* naked body. He was claiming her as Chris Anders never had. It was Chris's loss—one David was just as glad Chris was never likely to realize.

Shivers of delight shot through Emily as David's hands fondled her breasts, stroked her stomach, teased her thighs apart. She tried to lose herself completely in his touch, relish the sheer joy, but there were moments when she worried that he was inspecting, comparing. Finding her wanting?

She cursed Liza for having laid claim to David's heart. Would he ever be able to fully let her go? How was she ever to know the answer to that disturbing question? She sought solace in David's soft moans of pleasure as his lips traveled over her face and neck, his hands massaging the knobs of her spine. She was soothed as well as aroused by the whisper of her name on his lips. Her name, not Liza's. *My girlfriend and I . . .*

She arched, crying out David's name as he eased himself downward, his tongue lightly cruising across her stomach and then along the insides of her thighs. Her breath grew ragged, her fingers dug into his muscular back, as she ached to feel him inside her yet relished his desire not to rush the moment. For an instant she found herself wondering if Chris was as considerate and selfless a lover. Or was he a man driven more by his own need than his partner's?

David's artful lovemaking erased all questions about Chris—all thought totally from her mind. His kisses were demanding yet tender. She closed her eyes with a soft, ecstatic cry, her flat palms moving down his back and arms, over his firm, tight buttocks. Last time they'd lain naked together she hadn't realized how much his lean, muscular body was like an exquisite sculpture, full of deliciously smooth and rough planes, enthralling crevices.

She clutched at him as his ministrations escalated. His mouth and hands were relentless, giving a torturous pleasure that left her gasping.

"Please, David. Please . . ."

"Are you sure?"

"Yes. Yes."

"Tell me."

"I'm sure."

"Tell me you want me."

"I want you. I want you, David. . . ."

Her words were music to his ears. A heartbeat later, he entered her. Emily cried out with exhilaration as she felt him pulsing inside her, filling her. She felt intoxicated. Unlike the last time they'd made love, this time her intoxication had nothing to do with champagne. When she cried out in climax, his own joining hers moments later, she experienced a physical pleasure more intense than anything she had ever known.

LATER THAT NIGHT AS David lay sleeping, Emily remained awake, curled up beside him, her head propped up on his discarded pillow as well as her own. Moonlight drifted through the open, curtained window, bathing the room in a soft glow. As she solemnly studied the sleeping man, Emily no longer saw a friend, but a lover. A tender, sexy lover. Whatever happened from this point on, their easy friendship was gone forever. She felt a little sad and a little frightened. As tenuous as their friendship had been, their love affair might well turn out to be even more fragile.

Restless, Emily slipped out of bed, her bare feet making contact with some of David's photos on the carpet. She knelt down and carefully picked up the stack. They were spectacular. Collecting them all, she crossed the room to place them in David's open camera case, which rested on the desk by the window.

As she was placing the photos inside, another one caught her eye. As she lifted out the photo, her gaze remained fixed on it. It was an eight-by-ten glossy of a familiar-looking, exquisite dark-haired woman dressed in a jungle-print summer dress that showed off a lot of wonderful golden skin. It was signed. "To David. Now you can keep me near you always. Liza."

And he had done just that. Suddenly Liza's presence filled David's hotel room—crowding Emily out.

DAVID WAS FIRST disappointed then alarmed to find Emily gone when he woke up the next morning. For a moment he imagined it had all been a dream. A wonderful, incredible dream. He couldn't remember having spent a better night.

Fully awake now, he knew it was no dream. Something wonderful had happened between him and Emily last night. This morning he had none of the awkward, embarrassed, ashamed feelings he'd had the last time. This morning he wanted to enfold Emily in his arms and celebrate.

So where was she? He sat up, rubbing his eyes, smoothing back his tousled hair. He glanced around the room, checked out the bathroom. Only a scintillating hint of perfume remained. He reached for the phone, dialing Emily's hotel room. She answered on the first ring.

"Hi."

Her "hi" was bright. A little too bright. David got right to the point. "Why'd you leave?"

"I had to pack."

Definitely too bright. And not even a word about last night. Like nothing had happened. And why the sudden need to pack? He thought they weren't going to fly back till evening. What was going on? Regrets?

A sinking feeling made him clutch his stomach. What a fool to think one night of passion with him could eradicate Chris Anders from Emily's mind. Oh, she'd given it the old college try. He had to grant her that. Obviously it hadn't worked. Anger and disappointment tore at him, but he was damned if he was going to give Emily the satisfaction of knowing how much her rejection hurt. He dismissed the pain, telling himself it was nothing but male ego. An insult to his sexual prowess, that was all. Well, there were plenty of women out there eager to boost his ego. Women came on to him every day. Gorgeous models. Celebrities. The other night, Adrienne had sent out signals all evening. He'd ignored them because he didn't want to go to bed with Adrienne. He wanted to go to bed with Emily.

"If you want to stay up here longer, David, don't feel that you have to fly back with me. It's fine with me if you stay."

"Is it?"

Emily could hear the coolness in his voice. He wasn't even trying to coax her into staying. Was he just as glad she was going back? He made no mention of the plan they'd discussed on the flight up to Sacramento yesterday to rent a car and drive north into the mountains for a picnic before they took the shuttle flight back home. She'd been enthusiastic. Now her enthusiasm, like his, was gone. Along with her illusions.

"I've got piles of laundry and ironing waiting back home to catch up on." Emily hated herself for lying to David. What had happened to her vow of honesty? She knew what had happened to it. It had flown out the window when she saw Liza's photo. *Now you can keep me near you always. . . .*

"I might as well fly back with you," David said offhandedly. What fun was a picnic in the mountains alone? "I've got some things on a back burner I should attend to."

Emily picked up David's flat tone. He wasn't even making an effort to pretend that last night had meant something special to him. What did he want? A medal for honesty? Tears stung her eyes.

EMILY WAS WAITING for David down in the lobby, her suitcase at the side of the wing chair in which she was stiffly sitting, hands clasped. Her only hope at this point was that David would say nothing about what had happened between them last night. She wanted no lies, but she could only handle so much honesty.

Emily had her own succinct analysis. It had been a big mistake; that was all there was to it. It had been her fault. She knew that David was still struggling with his feelings for Liza. Hadn't he agreed that love wasn't like a faucet you could just turn off?

She almost lost her hard-won poise when she saw him stepping out of the elevator. He looked especially handsome this morning, casually dressed in jeans and a deep purple shirt, the cuffs rolled up. Jimmy Stewart on the range. His overnight case was slung over one shoulder, his camera case over the other. He didn't see her at first and she thought he looked a little lost. Poor, lost baby. It wasn't Emily's maternal instincts, however, that were stirred. It was pure lust.

She wanted to run over to him, drape her body around him and help him find his way. And maybe find hers in the process.

Then he saw her. The lost look was gone. He was clearly able to find his way on his own. His new expression was pleasant, cool, composed. She hated him for it, but she envied him, too.

He approached her with a purposeful stride. "I'll go settle the bill."

She got to her feet and grabbed hold of her suitcase, giving him a wide smile. "I did that already."

He was about to argue.

"You paid the fine." She hesitated, studiously avoiding his gaze. "Now we're even."

David hesitated, too. "Even," he echoed finally.

EMILY ATTEMPTED TO make small pleasantries on their way to the airport. David tried his best to do the same, but it was becoming increasingly difficult to conceal his upset. When they arrived at Departures, he slapped a bill in the cabbie's hand and was out the door before the taxi came to a full stop. Emily darted after him, charging into him as he came to a dead halt in the middle of the busy terminal.

She nearly lost her balance. "What's wrong? Did you forget something back at the hotel?"

He spun around and searched her face, prospecting for lies. "Are we just going to pretend nothing happened last night?"

Emily flushed. This wasn't exactly the time or place she would have chosen to discuss this extremely intimate topic. "I'm not pretending anything," she muttered, thinking that she was doing just the opposite—being realistic. "Couldn't we talk about this some other...?"

"When I go to bed with a woman, I like waking up beside her in the morning," David snapped.

Emily glared at him, forgetting about their very public surroundings. "You didn't the last time we slept together. You couldn't wait to get away."

"That was different and you know it. It's a pretty low blow to throw that at me."

Emily shrugged off his retort. "I don't want to fight with you, David. Last night—" She caught a nun's eye and flushed again.

"Do you have any complaints?" David charged, oblivious to onlookers.

"No. No complaints," Emily muttered, circling around him and heading for the shuttle gate for L.A.

David came up alongside her. "It's Chris, isn't it? You just can't let that jerk go."

Now it was Emily who stopped short. "Jerk? So, that's what you really think of Chris," she said accusingly.

David smiled sardonically. "That's just the tip of the iceberg. How you could put down someone like Neal Rickman and not see that he's a carbon copy of your dream boy..."

"And I suppose you think that vain, selfish, dumb model you dated the other night is any different from Liza?"

"Liza is not dumb."

"Two out of three doesn't win a prize in my book," she replied sarcastically.

David's features darkened. "You never understood Liza. You never understood me."

Emily fought back tears. "You're wrong. I understand you perfectly."

David wore a weary expression as she stormed off toward the gate. "Well, I wish I could say the same about you, Emily," he mumbled, disheartened.

"YOU'RE LATE," Naomi Bauer proclaimed as Emily stepped into her mother's apartment, a second-floor one-bedroom unit in a cluster development a few blocks from Studio City. A vast cry from the spacious garrison Colonial in Windsor, Connecticut, that she'd shared with her husband, Jason, for over twenty-five years. "Where were you all weekend? I left three messages for you."

"You left six messages," Emily said, stepping from the foyer into a box-shaped living room that smelled of lemon polish and was overstuffed with furnishings from the old house. Naomi didn't have an easy time parting with things she loved any more than she did people she loved.

Naomi followed her daughter into the living room. "So, where were you? Is it some big dark secret?"

Emily sank down on a tapestry couch that she used to pretend was the inside of a princess's coach when she was a child. "I was in Sacramento."

Naomi was nonplussed. "Sacramento? Why on earth would anyone go to Sacramento?"

"Good question."

"Seriously, Emily..."

Emily gave her mother a frank look. "Seriously, Mother, I went to Sacramento with David Turner for a romantic tryst. Oh, we told ourselves it was for a demonstration, but we knew that was just an excuse for hopping in the sack. We wanted to sleep together. We wanted..."

Naomi's face was bright red. "I didn't mean to pry."

"Yes, you did."

Naomi was taken aback by her daughter's rudeness. "This isn't like you, Emily."

Emily didn't know what had come over her. She was immediately contrite. "I'm sorry. I'm in a lousy mood. I shouldn't have come over for dinner tonight. I knew I'd be rotten company."

Naomi sat down in a brown corduroy wing chair, Jason Bauer's favorite. "Do you really care for this man, Emily?" She folded one hand over the other on her lap. "This . . . David?"

Emily smiled wanly. "At least you remembered his name."

"You know I worry that you'll settle . . ."

Something inside Emily snapped. "Don't worry, Mother. I'm not 'settling.' You don't have anything at all to worry about where me and what's-his-name are concerned. See, now you remember his name and I can't even keep track of it. That's how little he means to me. It was just a silly, inconsequential fling. Really, we would have both been better off if the cops had locked us up for the night. A night in jail would have been a lot smarter. . . ."

Naomi was aghast. "You and David were arrested? Good heavens, Emily, what for?"

Tears rolling down her face, Emily looked at her mother and started to laugh. "We got a little carried away at a demonstration."

Naomi stared at her daughter in shock. "Really, Emily."

Emily laughed harder, but it was bordering on hysteria. "Is it so awful to want to be loved exclusively? Why do I always have to share the men I love with someone else? And why does that someone else always have to be Liza?" By the time she was finished, Emily was crying in earnest.

Naomi Bauer crossed from her chair to the couch and put her arm around her daughter. "I know how much it hurts," she soothed, rocking her gently, tears springing to her eyes, too. "I know."

ALAN FREESE STUDIED the photos with interest. "This is some of your best work. Smart idea taking your muse with you up to Sacramento. You going to tell me what happened there between you and Emily?"

"You don't already know?"

"Cheryl couldn't get much out of Emily. Except there was some mention of getting arrested. So, I'm supposed to work on you."

"Forget it," David said sharply, gathering up the photos of the demonstration. He'd sent copies of these as well as the best of his others to three L.A.-based magazine groups. One of them, *Newsline*, had already responded. He had an interview set up for the first of the week. They'd sounded very interested. He should have been thrilled. Instead, he was left with an anticlimactic sort of feeling. Several times, he'd started to ring Emily up and tell her the good news. Wasn't this the kind of thing you shared with your best friend? Or your lover? Only now, it seemed, they were neither.

"Okay, okay, I can see the No Trespassing signs flashing," Alan teased, but then he grew serious. "Look, David, if there's something you want to talk about in confidence, I promise you it won't go beyond these four walls."

David was tucking his photos into a large manila envelope. He attended to the task with far more concentration than was necessary. Alan wandered over to David's fridge and got himself a beer, then sauntered back to the couch. David, at loose ends, was sifting through some fashion photos. He muttered something under his breath.

Alan leaned forward, resting his elbows on his thighs. "What was that?"

David looked up. "Women." His tone was partially scornful, partially perplexed.

Alan slumped back against the couch. "Ah."

David rubbed his face. He needed a shave. Maybe that's what he would do. He needed to do something. He needed to pull himself together. He needed to forget about Emily. Maybe he'd even give that men's group another try. Oh, they'd really have a field day with him now.

Alan took a slug of beer, then wiped his mouth with the back of his hand. "Well, at least she got your mind off Liza."

David's expression was doleful. "Believe me, it's no improvement."

"No, I didn't think it was," Alan admitted with a small smile.

David scowled at him. "I don't know up from down."

"None of us do."

David's scowl deepened. "That's no help."

"You want help? Call her."

David raised a hand in protest. "I can't."

"Why not?"

"Because I can't figure out what I want to say to her. I can't figure out what I want. What she wants. What makes sense."

"Making sense and being in love don't go together."

David eyed him sharply. "Who said anything about being in love? I don't even know if I like her." He sighed. "Well, okay, I like her. I have an . . . assortment of feelings for her. Not all of them good, by any means." He sighed. "Being in love with Liza was easy compared to this. At least I knew where Liza and I each stood. At different ends of the universe. Now, Emily and I . . . We seem to keep . . . tripping over each other."

Alan grinned. "Tripping? That's a new way of describing it."

David tossed a cushion at him.

EMILY GAVE CHERYL an expectant look as they strolled through Griffith Park on their lunch break. "You really think I have a shot?"

"Absolutely. Wasn't I the first one to tell you that article you wrote about the demonstration was terrific? It had such passion and intensity."

Well, she had to put those feelings someplace, Emily thought.

"Personally, I think you're wasted in editorial."

"I didn't think my résumé was all that impressive, though," Emily said.

"Obviously impressive enough to land you an interview."

Emily managed a smile. "It was exciting, though. Covering the story. Living dangerously." To put it mildly, she mused, thinking not of the demonstration or even the trip down to the police station, but those exhilarating hours spent with David in his hotel room. If only she hadn't come upon that photo of Liza. Then again, better to face reality sooner rather than later.

Cheryl poked her. "How am I going to survive at *Chic* without you?"

"I haven't gotten the job yet."

"You will. I can feel it in my bones." Cheryl gave her a studied look. "You want it, don't you?"

"Of course, I do."

"Then why aren't you more excited? Or should I guess?"

Emily scowled.

Cheryl's patience was wearing thin. "For God's sake, Emily, call David already. You know you're dying to tell him about your interview with *Newsline*. I bet if you asked him, he'd meet you over there and give you some moral support."

"I don't need moral support," Emily said tightly.

Cheryl regarded her friend skeptically. "Honey, you need at least that."

Emily started to argue until she felt the tears well in her eyes. "Men."

Cheryl grinned. "Tell me about it."

"I've lost my best friend. My best male friend," Emily quickly amended so as not to hurt Cheryl's feelings.

"I bet you could find him again if you looked hard enough."

Emily shook her head. "It isn't that simple."

"You mean you're not sure if it's a *friend* you're looking for."

Emily swiped at her teary eyes. "He carries a photo of Liza around with him."

"So? You've still got a photo of Chris on your desk at work. And umpteen others at home."

"That's different. I don't carry one around wherever I go. I certainly don't carry a photo of Chris with me when I go off to Sacramento with another man to . . . to demonstrate."

Cheryl's eyes sparkled. "'Demonstrate'? That's a quaint way of putting it."

Emily kicked a stone hard, forgetting she was wearing sandals. She flinched, then decided her painful toe was a distraction from her aching heart.

8

EMILY WAS A NERVOUS wreck as she pulled into the parking lot
of an imposing thirty-story office building on Wilshire Bou-
levard, the top five floors housing the prestigious West Coast
offices of *Newsline* magazine. A sudden flash of lightning
zigzagged down from the sky as she got out of her car. It was
a long walk from the parking lot to the building. She hadn't
even brought a raincoat. If there was a downpour before she
made it to the lobby, she'd arrive at her interview looking like
a drowned rat.

She managed to get to the building right before the clouds
burst open. The rainy season had come to L.A. Emily hated
the rain, especially in L.A., where it was inevitably accom-
panied by mud slides all over the city. Every time she turned
on the TV there'd be news and film clips of houses slipping
down canyons. Not that she watched much television. She'd
even been weaning herself off "Sports Beat," Chris's nightly
show. She was down to once a week. Now, when she watched
Chris on the tube, instead of sitting there teary-eyed and depressed, she felt more wistful and even found herself trying
to sort out how she really felt about him. She wasn't sure. She
wasn't sure of anything these days.

Except that she wanted a job at *Newsline*.

As she rode the elevator, her hands went to the string of
pearls around her neck, kneading them like worry beads. She
wished now she had called David, knowing that if she'd had
the courage to ask him to meet her over here and give her
some moral support before the interview, he would have

come. Apart from everything else that had gone on between them, she never doubted that if she reached out to him as a friend, he would respond. He would be there for her.

Which was why her mouth dropped open when the elevator doors slid apart and she saw David sitting in a cocoa-brown leather chair a few feet away from *Newsline*'s reception desk. ESP? Or had Cheryl taken it upon herself to call him?

Neither, she realized, if David's startled expression when he saw her step out of the elevator, was any indication. He looked as surprised to see her as she was to see him.

What gives? they were both thinking. There were other thoughts, too. Like how much they missed each other, how good they each thought the other looked, how miserable they'd been since their angry parting.

David rose from his chair as she approached. They watched each other with puzzled expressions, cautious, neither of them wanting to give too much away.

When they were within touching distance, Emily came to a stop, the light dawning now that the shock of seeing him was wearing off. "You've got an interview here, too?" Brilliant deduction. Who was acting dumb now?

"With Evan Hoopes. Eleven o'clock."

"I've got an eleven o'clock with Roger Bagley."

Neither of them could drag their eyes away from the other.

Emily sucked in a shaky breath. "Well... Good luck." She didn't extend her hand. She didn't think she could touch him without setting off sparks, and she did have an interview to get through.

"You, too." David's hands remained at his sides. Like they were glued there.

They thought about smiling at each other, but both felt restrained; afraid of rejection.

Emily went over to the reception desk to check in. The receptionist asked her to have a seat. There were plenty to choose from in the spacious gray-and-peach reception room. After a moment's hesitation, Emily chose the one next to David.

"I'm nervous as hell," she confided, picking up a magazine from the glass-and-wrought-iron coffee table, not opening it.

"That makes two of us."

She tested out a tentative smile on him.

He smiled back. And let his gaze drift down her trim body clad in a stylish navy-and-white tweed double-breasted blazer over a navy skirt and simple white silk blouse, a single strand of pearls around her neck. "I like the suit. Very editorial."

She laughed softly, giving him a closer scrutiny—or at least a more obvious one. He was wearing pleated khaki trousers, a blue-black sport jacket, a teal-blue shirt and a blue-and-tan Paisley tie. His dark hair was brushed back off his face and teased the back of his collar. David eschewed trends in dress, and had an individual style. Casual but strong. He looked very handsome. "You look like an up-and-coming photojournalist."

Now that they had accepted each other's best wishes and compliments graciously, they found themselves at a loss about where to go from there. Emily once again fidgeted with her pearls with an electric nervousness that wasn't due to the interview anymore. David interlocked his fingers, pressed his palms together and stared blankly at a Matisse poster on the peach-tinted wall across from him. The air around them felt charged.

Emily checked her watch. "It's five after eleven."

David did a recheck of his watch. "I've got only two minutes after." He smiled. "Digital."

She glanced at his watch and nodded.

David unclasped his fingers, turning abruptly to her. He exhaled and his breath fluttered her hair. "I wanted to call you."

"You did?" She stared down at her hands resting on the unopened magazine in her lap, but she could feel his eyes on her.

"I wanted to apologize for that scene I made at the airport, Emily. My outburst was . . . uncalled-for." He spoke rapidly and kept his voice very low so he wouldn't be overheard by the receptionist.

"I wanted to call you, too." Before she got the chance to say why—just as well, since she wasn't really sure why—the receptionist called out her name.

"Mr. Bagley will see you now, Ms. Bauer. It's the second office on the right, through the double doors."

As she started to rise, David impulsively stuck out his hand. Emily clasped it like a lifeline. "Good luck," he mouthed with a tender smile.

She walked through the double doors, enervated. She had her friend back. The rest remained to be seen.

"I SENSED A REAL NICE interplay going on there." Bagley, a broadly built man with red hair and muscular freckled arms bent forward at his desk, as if poised for motion, and looked from Emily to the copy and photograph grouping in front of him—her story on the demonstration, and David's photos.

"Yes," Emily said, clearing her throat. "The pictures do highlight very dramatically what I was trying to get across in print."

Bagley cocked his head as he looked over at her. "I was talking about you and the photographer."

Emily felt her face warm. She dropped her gaze. "Oh. Well . . ."

"You complement each other. You must know that already yourself. Compatible styles. A certain simpatico. Have you covered other stories together?"

"No. No, this was the first . . ." Before she could go on to explain that this was her first real hard-news article ever, Bagley interrupted.

"Not the last, though," he said with a wink. "I'm not the sort of employer to mince words, Ms. Bauer. We like your style here at *Newsline*. You know how to draw people out. And you know how to get what you hear down on paper. If all the details can be ironed out satisfactorily, we want you and Turner on our team."

"Me and Turner?"

"Not to say we want the two of you joined at the hip. There'll be plenty of solo assignments for each of you and other matchups, but we here at *Newsline* are very tuned in to solid pairings. Am I right about you and Turner?"

Emily could think of nothing else to say or do other than nod, the whole time wondering how David was reacting to the same pitch from Hoopes across the hall.

Emily cleared her throat. "I was really hoping, as I wrote in my covering letter, to get into the editorial department as quickly as possible," Emily said hoarsely. "Most of my experience at *Chic* has been as an editor."

Bagley smiled. "We'll have you do some editorial work in good time, Ms. Bauer. We like to put our new people on the front lines for a while. Especially ones who write as well as you do."

Emily felt a little thrill at the compliment. It didn't really distress her to think about covering other stories. Something else was distressing her, though.

"What if David...Mr. Turner...doesn't take the job?" she asked nervously. Thinking about the mayhem she'd caused David at the demonstration and everything that had resulted, Emily couldn't help but be skeptical of David's desire to hook up with her on future stories here at *Newsline.* Would he accept the job—even what had to be a job of a lifetime—under those terms?

Bagley assured her that her appointment wasn't contingent upon David accepting a position at *Newsline.* "However, I can't see him turning it down," he added confidently.

Emily wasn't nearly as confident as Bagley. She also wasn't sure how it would be for her to work closely with David, now that their relationship was so ephemeral.

EMILY KNEW, AFTER SHE and Bagley shook on the deal, that she would wait for David to finish his interview. She had to know his reaction. Had he signed on as willingly as she had? As she approached the double doors leading back into the reception area she tried to steel herself for the answer, admitting that she would feel awful and guilty if he turned the job down because of her.

David was already out there, waiting for her, his interview having concluded minutes earlier. The bright smile on his face immediately told her what she needed to know. Her smile in response gave him his.

A wave of relief wafted over both of them.

They hurried out into the hallway like fugitives on the run, embracing without artifice or awkwardness as they got to the elevator.

"I can't believe it!" Emily gasped.

"Neither can I," David said, beaming. "I have you to thank, you know."

"Oh, you would have gotten the job whether or not I'd written the article."

"No, I don't mean that," he replied softly. "I mean that you believed in me. Encouraged me."

"You did the same for me," she murmured.

He leaned forward slightly, his gaze steady on her.

"This calls for a celebration," he whispered. "Do you want to?"

"Yes," she whispered back and licked her dry lips.

THEY HURRIED THROUGH THE rain-drenched parking lot to David's car. Emily got in without argument. She was afraid that if they drove separately, one or the other of them might change their mind. She'd deal with her car tomorrow.

Once they were settled in David's car, Emily searched his face almost imploringly. His tender smile was all the reassurance she needed that they were doing the right thing.

As the rain beat down on the car, the sound filling their heads, David pulled her to him and kissed her with a hunger that had been churning inside him for weeks.

"I missed you," he said and meant it. He had almost forgotten how good she felt in his arms, how delicious her lips were to kiss. He marveled at the fact that while Emily was not a classic beauty à la Liza, her features held for him a uniquely tantalizing and precious attraction.

They began kissing again, more intently, getting lost in it, but then Emily reluctantly pulled away.

"What if Hoopes or Bagley comes out and sees us?"

David grinned. "Right. Now that we're working together we've got to show proper decorum."

"Absolutely."

"Definitely."

One more heart-stopping kiss and David was peeling out of the parking lot. He put on the defroster, the windows having silvered with their breathing.

THEY FELL INTO EACH OTHER'S arms as soon as they entered David's loft. His hands shook as he unbuttoned her blouse. He slipped it off her, his palms skimming lightly down her shoulders. Emily shivered at his touch and smiled tremulously.

"Oh, David, I feel like this is a whole new start for us."

He pulled her to him and kissed her, needily, whispering. "Yes, yes. A whole new beginning."

Impatient to begin, Emily hurriedly stripped off the rest of her clothes, not provocatively but eagerly, which David found all the more sensual. He was out of his own clothes in two seconds flat—except for his socks. They both giggled as she knelt at his feet and helped him off with them.

Their giggles came to an abrupt halt when Emily stayed put on her knees, trailing her lips up his thigh. The heat of her breath made David tremble, and he gasped in earnest when he felt her slowly, erotically drawing him into her mouth. Pulsating heat suffused him—and sensations almost too much to bear. He pulled in his breath, arched his head, and gripped her shoulders to keep from swaying. Spirals of pleasure swirled through his entire body with each swipe of her tongue.

Emily had never before felt so free, so abandoned, so bold in her lovemaking. Something inside her had changed—was changing still. She felt a new recklessness of the heart. Everything seemed new to her. A whole new start, a whole new her, a whole new relationship. . . .

Finally he pulled her up to him, kissing her fiercely, the intermingling of tastes driving them both wild.

"You feel so silky," she murmured in a husky voice against his lips. Her hand slipped down between them to where her mouth had been, enfolding him, feeling him quiver, her own body feeling shock waves of desire. When their lips parted, she stared into his face, her eyes huge and liquid with lust.

He smiled tenderly, swooping his head down and parting his lips to draw in one nipple, then the other. Her scent was strong and sweet, bringing back in a flash memories of their previous shared intimacies as if they were a small but rare collection of precious photographs.

He gathered her in his arms, but instead of carrying her off to his bed across the loft he carried her a few yards away to what had been a beach-scene backdrop for some fashion shots he'd taken the previous day. A lush burgundy velour blanket was spread over soft, white sand, a bright teal-and-white umbrella shading the sunbathing model from the make-believe sun.

The setting might have been pure fantasy, but the feelings Emily and David were experiencing were poignantly real. As he laid her down on the blanket and stretched out beside her, curving her against him, Emily felt as though they were on a glorious tropical island of their own making. They basked in the dappling heat radiating from their bodies, passing back and forth from one to the other.

Was this love? The question flitted through Emily's mind. She wasn't certain. All she was certain of was that there was no artifice between them. She and David knew each other for who they were, for what they felt, for what they'd been through in the past. And she knew they wanted each other. Maybe that was enough for now. There'd be time later on for them to label their feelings, weigh them against the other ones they'd carried around for so long.

As David began to explore her body with his large, warm, competent hands, all thought evaporated. She pressed against him hard, urging their union. No, not union—re-union. The thought made her smile. David kissed her smiling lips and entered her at the same time in one long, heated slide that brought tears to the corners of her eyes.

She closed around him, firmly but gently, full of quivering responses that drove him to step up the rhythm. Emily, once the girl with two left feet when it came to dancing, followed his beat to perfection.

At first she thought she was simply hearing bells. The sound mingled quite musically with their cries of release. Then David rolled off her, groaning.

"Damn. It's my phone." Reluctantly, he rose, stepping off the blanket onto the sand, and reached out for the unwelcome intruder. His voice was husky as he said a brusque "Hello."

His back was to Emily who was lying on her side studying his lean, naked body with glutted pleasure—until she saw his whole body go rigid. And then she heard the fateful word and her whole body went numb.

"Liza."

David spoke her name as if he were addressing a visiting dignitary. Or maybe a goddess. Gone was the brusque tone. There was awe in his voice, but Emily also detected a hint of alarm and embarrassment.

"Doing?" There was a long pause. He didn't turn to look at Emily. "Nothing much."

He sounded to Emily like a man caught in the act of adultery. She sat up, suddenly cold and feeling very exposed. She draped part of the blanket around her. The "sun" had suddenly gone behind a large black cloud. She listened sharply to David's end of the conversation, which was quite terse.

After a long silence, he said, "What?"

Emily could hear the surprise in his voice.

"When?" His pitch rose a little.

Emily got colder. She rose, draping the blanket around her, and sat down on a stool that allowed her to view David in profile.

His features were strained. She watched him run his fingers absently through his tousled hair. Only minutes ago it had been her fingers. Somehow it felt like a lifetime ago.

"Emily?"

Emily raised a brow. Liza was asking about her?

"No. No, she's not at home. As a matter of fact . . . she's right here."

Emily saw him glance over his shoulder at the "beach scene" only to find her and the blanket gone. His eyes searched her out quickly enough. He gave her a pained smile.

"We were . . . celebrating." His tone, however, sounded funereal. "We both landed jobs at *Newsline* magazine." There was a brief pause. "No, I know you didn't know we were both looking to get out of the fashion industry. Yes. Yes, it is a surprise."

Emily smiled wryly. Liza was in for quite a few surprises. Little did Emily know that so was she.

"No. No, we were just . . . having a drink. Sure. Sure, I'll put her on."

Emily glared at him. Having a drink! She waved the phone away, shaking her head vigorously. She couldn't bear to speak to Liza at this particular moment. She had a few choice words for David, though.

David put the phone back to his ear. "She just stepped into the bathroom." He smoothed back his hair again. "Yes, yes, I'll tell her." He rubbed his jaw. "Yes, yes, I'm sure she will." He pressed his temple. "Me? Of course, I'm delighted," he said, grim-faced. "No, I think I can work that out. Speak to you soon."

When he dropped the receiver into the cradle, the sound had a surprisingly resounding effect. Something akin to a death knell. He stared at Emily for several moments before speaking.

"They're coming back."

Emily blinked several times. "For a visit?"

David shook his head.

Emily's hand absently let go of the blanket. It slipped off her shoulders as she gasped, "For good?"

"Liza says she and Chris both decided they hate New York and they want out of the rat race. They want to be back in sunny California. Chris has already lined up a sportscasting job with a local affiliate and Liza's taking an offer as a designer for a bathing-suit company down in Santa Monica."

Emily sat there on the stool, naked and speechless.

"She wanted me to tell you that she and Chris are relying on us to give them the moral support they're going to need to make such a dramatic switch."

Emily swallowed hard. "When?" It was a wonder she could get that much out.

"Saturday."

"This Saturday?"

David nodded. "Liza asked if I could pick them up at LAX."

"And you agreed."

David frowned. "Did you want me to say no?"

Emily didn't know what she wanted—any more than she knew what the two of them were doing having this discussion with each other in their birthday suits!

Without a word, she retrieved the blanket and hopped off the stool, heading for her clothes. David intercepted her before she got to them.

"Emily, nothing's changed." His tone, however, didn't jibe with his words.

"I'm not saying it has." Emily didn't have to say it.

"Okay," he conceded. "It'll be an adjustment."

"Please let me get dressed, David. Right now, I want to put my clothes on and go home," she said plaintively.

David didn't release her. "What if it had been Chris calling you? If he'd asked what you and I were doing, would you have gone into details? Would you have turned him down if he'd asked you to pick them up at the airport?"

"I'm not sure." Her words came out sounding as confused as she felt. She gave him a dark look. "Is that all we were doing here today, David? Having a drink?"

"What did you want me to tell her?" David asked, fired up.

"Not that we were . . . having a drink."

"Do you want me to call her back? Tell her she interrupted us in the throes of passion? If that's what you want, Emily . . ."

"I already told you what I want," she said quietly. "I want to get dressed and go home."

David still wouldn't let her go. "Her call caught me off guard."

"So I noticed."

"I didn't know how to tell her."

"Or maybe you didn't want to."

"Emily . . ."

"Tell me one thing. Tell me you still don't have feelings for her. Tell me you're not still in love with her."

"That's two things."

"Okay, answer the second."

David released her. "Emily, we're standing here naked. We've just had some of the best sex we've ever had. Go on, deny it."

Emily fought back tears. "I'm not going to deny it. But I happen to think that having sex and making love are two different things."

"Not where you're concerned they aren't," he said gently. "Ask me how I feel about you, Emily."

She closed her eyes. "I . . . can't. First I need to know how you feel about Liza."

"Two can play the same game. How do you feel about Chris?"

"It isn't a game, David."

"Are you still in love with him?"

"I don't know how I feel about Chris," Emily admitted honestly. "I haven't seen him in a . . . long time."

He smiled tenderly. "Okay, so neither of us is going to win any prizes at the moment for sorting out our feelings. We'll give it a little time. We'll see them and then . . ."

"I imagine you'll be seeing a lot more of Liza than I will of Chris." She could bet there wouldn't be a message from him waiting for her on her answering machine when she got home. He'd left it up to Liza to pass on the news.

"I have an idea. We'll pick Chris and Liza up together. How about that?"

Emily managed a dull nod. "If that's what you want."

"That's what I want," he said, sealing his affirmation with a kiss—a kiss that both of them noticed lacked all the heat and fire of their earlier ones.

They gathered up their clothes and dressed quickly, awkwardly. Undressing earlier, they had feasted on each other. Now they kept their eyes averted.

Chris and Liza were coming back. So much for "out of sight, out of mind." Try as they might to deny it, both to themselves and to each other, Emily and David knew that the return of their prodigal "lovers" would impact sharply on their relationship even if they didn't yet know in what way.

NAOMI BAUER SHOWED UP at her daughter's door minutes after Emily arrived home from David's loft. She entered in a flurry, waving a newspaper in Emily's face.

"Did you hear from him? Do you know?" she demanded excitedly, unbuttoning her raincoat.

"About Chris coming back to L.A.?"

"I told you the man didn't look right. I knew something was brewing. It's just like I said—"

"He's not coming back alone, Mother. He's bringing his wife."

Naomi gave Emily's comment an idle shrug. "You wait and see. I won't say another word."

Emily only wished that were true.

"Did you read it in the paper?" her mother quizzed.

"No."

"Chris called you?"

"No. Liza called. Actually, she called David." A weary smile popped up on Emily's lips. "I almost forgot. I got the job at *Newsline*. So did David."

Naomi hesitated. "That's good, dear." The lack of enthusiasm in her tone belied her congratulations.

Emily knew that her mother thought working at *Chic* was far more *chic* than working at a magazine that focused on hard news. She also knew her mother thought she had a better chance of attracting glamorous men if she worked in a glamorous setting.

"They want me to do more reporting. Bagley thinks I've got a nice writing style. I'll be teaming up with David on some stories. He'll be the eyes, I'll be the ears." An hour ago the prospect of working together had been exhilarating, seductive—traveling the globe together, making love on real beaches. . . .

What would it be like now? Would they ever be able to recapture the feelings that had literally swamped them when they flew out of the *Newsline* offices that afternoon? When they'd talked about this being a whole new start for their relationship, they certainly hadn't factored in the return of Chris and Liza. How would David feel when he saw his old love again? How would she feel when she saw Chris?

"Dear, your answering machine is blinking. Should I flick it on for you?"

Emily gave a distracted nod, barely listening. At first.

Within seconds, she was all ears.

"Hi, Em. It's me, Chris. Just wanted to let you know I'm coming home. L.A., that is. It's been a long time. I can't wait to see you again, Em. I'll be back on Saturday and I'll give you a buzz. We've got to get together. See ya soon, babe. And I haven't forgotten our dinner date at Spago's."

The machine clicked off. Emily sat down. She gave her mother a dazed look. Naomi was smiling. It looked more like gloating. "Did you hear? Not *we're* coming home, *I'm* coming home. You mark my words, there's trouble brewing in paradise. And who's the first one he calls?"

"Really, Mother, I'm far from the first one he called. It's in today's paper."

"That was a professional announcement. Probably put in by his press agent. The phone call was *personal*."

Emily couldn't dismiss her mother's interpretation of the message. The whole timbre of Chris's voice had altered; an unexpected shift from the casual almost-professional voice she was so familiar with—his "television voice," she called it—to one decidedly more...personal, just as her mother had said. There was even—dared she think it?—a touch of intimacy in his tone. Even . . . even a touch of eagerness.

Eagerness. She couldn't believe it. Chris eager to see her? Her mother was probably right. He and Liza must be having problems. The first year of marriage was always a period of adjustment. He probably just wanted his old pal *Em's* trusty shoulder to lean on.

What if it was more than that? What if . . . ?

Emily stood abruptly. She thought about her fight with David over Liza. Suddenly the shoe was on the other foot. Pinching badly.

9

AIRPORTS WERE DEFINITELY not a great relationship booster, Emily grimly concluded. If things had gone poorly with David at that terminal in Sacramento, things were going from bad to worse at LAX. Not that they were fighting. Not even that they weren't speaking to each other. It was worse. They were back to being disgustingly *civil*. And banal.

"Why is it, when you're departing, yours is always the plane that's delayed, and when you're waiting for an arrival, it's always the plane you're waiting for that's behind schedule?"

Emily regarded David in silence for a moment and then said in a monotone, "All planes are late."

He produced a loopy sort of smile. "I suppose you're right."

Emily shifted in the uncomfortable sea-blue plastic seat in the waiting area. She wished now she hadn't agreed to come along to the airport, but she wasn't really sure which was troubling her most—this awkward waiting time alone with David, watching David when he greeted Liza, or her greeting Chris with David watching. More than likely, it was a combination of all three.

"An awful lot of incoming flights," David muttered, staring up at the arrivals board.

"Outgoing, too," Emily mumbled, her gaze fixing for several moments on the departures board. She started counting the departures. It gave her something to do; something to occupy her mind. It didn't work. She kept wondering what was occupying David's mind. A part of her wanted to turn to him, throw her arms around him and say, *Let's get out of here. Chris and Liza can take a cab. Let's go back to your loft and make passionate love on your make-believe beach. Let's make believe nothing's changed. If we make believe long enough and hard enough, maybe it'll come true.*

Instead, she said, "Three departures to Chicago alone."

And David said, "I've never been to Chicago."

"Neither have I."

"The Windy City."

Emily gave him a distracted glance. "What?"

"Chicago. The Windy City."

"Oh. Right." And she thought to herself, *This is so dumb*.

David was thinking much the same thing. He hated the archness that had snapped into their relationship. He hated all the repercussions and ramifications of that fateful phone call from Liza three days ago. Here he was, sitting beside a woman he was crazy about. So why couldn't he just turn to her and tell her, *Emily, I'm crazy about you?* Because in fourteen minutes and twenty seconds, give or take a couple of seconds, another woman whom he'd been wildly, insanely, ridiculously in love with for over twenty-five years was going to burst through those swinging double doors and he didn't know how seeing her was going to affect him.

As if that wasn't worrisome enough, there was the not-so-small matter of how Emily was going to feel when she saw Chris again. How would a few months of friendship with him—albeit with some hearty dollops of passion thrown in—stack up against a love that had burned inside her since childhood? Chris was charismatic, urbane, looked like a million bucks, and carried himself like the second coming of Cary Grant. Did he even stand a ghost of a chance when compared to the Adonis sportscaster?

Emily's voice cut through his ruminations. "They changed the board. The plane's landing. Must have had good winds."

Nothing but ill winds here, she thought, her anxiety heightening. And her anxiety had been pretty high to begin with.

David inhaled, exhaled, then forgot to breathe for almost a minute. His palms were sweaty, his muscles taut.

"Do you know where they're going to be staying?"

David looked at Emily with a blank expression. "No. Liza didn't say."

"Neither did Chris."

The blank look was instantly gone from David's face. "You heard from Chris?"

"Sort of," Emily hedged, not sure why she was hedging.

David didn't let it go. "What does 'sort of' mean? You either heard from him or you didn't hear from him."

"Why are you so angry?"

"I'm not angry. I merely asked a question," he said defensively, knowing full well it wasn't anger but jealousy. Why had Chris suddenly decided to get in touch with Emily? She'd led him to believe that in the past she'd always been the one to make the overtures.

"He left a message for me on my answering machine. All right?"

"Did he say anything . . . special?"

Emily bit back a smile, realizing with a spark of pleasure that David was jealous. "Just that he was coming back and was looking forward to seeing me again. Oh, and that he hasn't forgotten our date at Spago's," she said airily, even though inwardly she felt a little twinge of shame for deliberately encouraging David's jealousy. On the other hand, she was feeling so vulnerable that she had to do something.

"What date?"

Emily's gaze slid from David to fix on the swing doors leading into the waiting area. "Passengers are starting to come out." The voice that came from her dry throat sounded raspy.

Both of them rose, rooted to their spots, trying desperately to look nonchalant and not succeeding at all well.

Liza swept in a few steps ahead of a small group of Japanese businessmen, moving with her characteristic impatience. Chris wasn't yet in sight, so Emily's attention was fully drawn to her ex-roommate who had stolen the heart of the man of her dreams. She supposed she ought to make that *men*. Liza's dark hair still hung halfway down her back in lustrous waves. Her wide-set eyes were as riveting a violet as she remembered, her ivory skin as flawless as ever. If anything, her style of dress was even more exotic and provocative than ever—this time, a clinging lime-colored Lycra bodysuit under an open Chinese-print silk tunic of vibrant rainbow hues. From the look of it, she hadn't gained a single ounce. *Damn her.*

Emily could hear David suck in a slow breath as Liza, after cruising the crowd, spotted them, gave an elegant wave and hurried over. She slowed a few feet from them, smiling sultrily. Giving Emily a quick wink, she turned her full attention on David as if he were the only living creature in the whole bustling terminal.

"David," Liza murmured in her breathy, vibrant voice, stretching her arms out wide.

Emily could feel David's indecision and uneasiness as if it were her own. She couldn't stand it. She gave him a little shove, immediately regretting it as she watched the pair embrace—David awkwardly, Liza distressingly enthusiastically. Emily was so absorbed by their display of affection that she didn't see Chris until he was practically on top of her.

"Autograph hounds," he said with the roguish smile she remembered so well. Then, to Emily's astonishment, he pulled her into his arms and gave her a big kiss. On the lips. When he released her, Emily was bright red. She glanced over at David. His coloring was equally vivid.

Liza gave her a rushed squeeze and a kiss that landed in the air in the general vicinity of her cheek. "So, what's the word on you two?" Liza demanded, arms akimbo as she eyed David with a tantalizing smile. "Are you an item or what?"

Or what was right, David and Emily were both thinking, but were saved by Chris from saying anything aloud.

"Put them on the spot, why don't you?" he muttered, giving his wife of five months a less-than-adoring look.

"I don't know why it bugs you so much that I'm direct and to the point," she snapped back at her husband.

Emily and David exchanged glances. There was "trouble in River City," all right. With a capital *T*.

"Let's get out of here before I've got a horde of fans swarming over me," Chris said tightly.

Liza slipped her arm possessively through David's. "A swarm. If he hadn't told that stewardess on board who he was, and she hadn't spread it around, no one would have paid any attention to him." She pressed her hand dramatically to her chest. "Heaven forbid."

Chris scowled at her and looked about to tell her off when he abruptly shifted gears, turning away from Liza and sweeping an arm around Emily's shoulder as they started for the exit.

"So, Em. What do you think of this move?" he asked jauntily.

Even though David was a few paces ahead of her with Liza, Emily knew he'd be able to pick up their conversation.

"If it's what you want, Chris . . . You and Liza . . ."

"It goes beyond that," he said rather mysteriously.

They were passing the escalator that led down to the baggage-claim area.

"What about your luggage?" Emily asked.

"We sent it all ahead," Chris replied. "I hate coping with baggage and all that."

"Sent it where?" David asked as they all reached the glass exit doors.

"Oh, we arranged to lease this nifty house in Newport Beach," Liza said enthusiastically. "Wait till you guys see it. You're going to love it."

"You've seen it?" Emily asked.

Liza smiled coquettishly. "Before Chris and I got really serious, I dated an artist who was leasing the place. You remember him, don't you, Em? Andrew Miller."

Emily bristled at Liza using the nickname Chris had given her. She also found it hard to believe that Liza had had time to fit in any dates with another man before she and Chris got serious, considering how "serious" they looked that first night she'd spied them devouring each other on the couch.

"No, sorry," she said. "I don't remember him."

Liza grinned. "No wonder. His house might have been memorable, but its tenant was a first-class jerk. And, personally, I never thought he had an ounce of talent. Anyway, when I finally convinced Chris that we had to move back here—"

"Hold on," Chris broke in indignantly. "You didn't have to *convince* me. I wanted to come back as much as you did. There was a small matter of a contract that I had to figure a way out of."

"Fine," Liza said curtly, turning her attention back to David. "Anyway, I called this real-estate agent out here, and offhandedly asked about the place. I couldn't believe my luck when she said it was available."

"What happened to the artist?" Emily asked.

Liza shrugged. "He's painting in some garret in Paris, last I heard."

"Selling the paintings Liza thought stank for about fifty grand apiece," Chris said dryly. "There was a big spread on him in the *New York Times* magazine section a couple of months ago. Universal raves from the critics. But then, what do critics know."

"Not very much," Liza said snippily. "Or so you said when you read Calhoun's review of your show in the *Manhattan Press*."

The sparring between the newlyweds didn't come to a halt until they got to David's car. The respite turned out to be strictly temporary.

Liza effectively edged Emily out of the way as her hand darted for the door handle to the front passenger's seat. "You don't mind, do you, Emily? I get carsick when I sit in the back. Isn't that true, David?"

David obviously hadn't the faintest idea, but he nodded weakly, avoiding Emily's gaze.

Without a word, Emily climbed in back beside Chris. How many times in the past would this seating arrangement have suited her just fine? At that particular moment, the past seemed a long time ago.

"You never got carsick in New York riding in the back of limos," Chris remarked with a wry smile that didn't reach his eyes.

Liza gave a nonchalant shrug. "Limos are different."

The bickering did finally stop when they got on the freeway to Newport Beach. It was replaced by Liza punctuating the intermittent tense silences with anecdotes of life's ups and downs in New York's fast lane. After about twenty minutes of "entertainment," Chris sank his head wearily against the side window and clutched Emily's hand.

"God, it's good to be back." He sighed dramatically.

Emily stared at their entwined hands as if she were seeing some kind of vision. When was the last time she and Chris had held hands like this? Actually, she couldn't think of a time. She was pretty sure this was a first. Her luck—she'd had to wait until he got married. But that wasn't the only reason

Emily couldn't enjoy the moment. She was preoccupied with the duo in the front seat. She found it positively disgusting how David was hanging on to Liza's every word, laughing at all her dumb stories, relishing every touch—of which there were quite a few. Every time Liza came to a punch line, she'd stroke David's shoulder or ruffle his hair or give his arm a little squeeze. How come, all of a sudden, she couldn't keep her hands off him? Maybe, Emily mused, Liza just couldn't stand the thought that the man who'd carried a torch for her all these years was now burning with desire for someone else. Or, at least, that was the way it had been until Liza decided to pop back into their lives.

"A positively ghastly individual," Liza was drawling. "I don't care how many books he's written or how many appearances he's made on the morning talk-show circuit. The man's a pompous ass."

Chris leaned closer to Emily. "She's peeved because he told her one of her designs reminded him of those bedraggled costumes the 'flower children' of the sixties used to wear."

"I heard that," Liza said curtly. "I don't think that remark was called for." They could all hear the note of hurt in her voice.

Chris smiled contritely. "You're right. Sorry."

There was a long, uncomfortable silence. It was Chris who came to the rescue. He leaned forward, affectionately tousling his wife's hair. "If we're going to talk about pompous asses, let's tell them about that ridiculous sculptress who specialized in, shall we say, particular male anatomical parts."

Liza trilled a laugh. David had always loved Liza's laugh. It had such a sultry, provocative quality. He couldn't help himself. Something unbidden stirred in one of *his* "particular anatomical parts." At the same time, though, he was acutely aware of Emily and Chris snuggled together in the back seat. Oh, there was nothing overtly seductive in Chris's manner, but he was certainly acting more buddy-buddy with Emily than David would have expected—at least from what Emily had told him about their "ultraplatonic" relationship. Had she told him everything?

He glanced in his rearview mirror, catching an unguarded look at Emily who seemed to him to be feasting her eyes on Chris, hanging on to his every word, practically wallowing in his attentions. David felt a flicker of rage. He forgot all about the effect Liza's laugh had had on him.

"Let's pick up some barbecue after we're settled and we'll all have dinner together," Liza said gaily, resting her hand lightly on David's knee. "You're still wild about barbecued ribs, aren't you?"

David was astonished that Liza even knew he loved ribs. She had always seemed so oblivious to his likes and dislikes.

He never told me he loved barbecued ribs, Emily thought sulkily. *And here I'd deluded myself into thinking we'd shared so much about ourselves. I don't really know David at all.*

"I remember this wonderful little take-out rib place not far away. After we check on the house and make sure everything's in order, we can take a run over there," Liza was saying. "We'll have a picnic on the beach and watch the sunset together. What could be more perfect?"

David and Emily could have thought of any number of things. They spoke at the same time, begging off with limp excuses that Liza and Chris quickly overrode. They both were quite insistent about them staying. Emily and David formed the same conclusion. It was as if the pair didn't want to be alone.

Once the plans were set, Liza and Chris mellowed out. The same couldn't be said of David and Emily. The prospect of the foursome spending the evening together did not sit well with either of them. It mightn't have been so bad if Chris and Liza

had been acting in character. Only they weren't. Before they'd
left L.A. for Manhattan, the newlyweds had been so thor-
oughly absorbed in each other that they had never even noticed if David or Emily were around. They might have been
sticks of furniture, part of the woodwork. If it had been disturbing not to be noticed, however, being noticed was prov-
ing even more alarming.

David and Emily were glad when they finally arrived at the
house; the close confines of the car had only added to their
anxiety. They piled out after David pulled into the stone
driveway of a small but charming Mediterranean-style per-
simmon-colored stucco villa that overlooked the blue Pa-
cific. Liza sidled over to her husband who was surveying the
place with a clear look of pleasure.

"I told you it was terrific," she said, slipping an arm around
his waist. "Our first real home. I refuse to count that roach-
infested apartment on the East Side that we lived in for the
last three months."

Chris gave her a skewed glance. "Roach infested? You saw
one roach."

"In the oven. Trying to make time with my roast duck."

Liza gave an expressive little shiver of revulsion and everyone laughed. For a minute Chris and Liza sounded like a
comedy team. Emily and David secretly hoped they would
keep it up. A few laughs, some barbecue, a little wine, and
they could make their escape. Then again, neither of them
was particularly looking forward to the long drive back to
L.A. alone together—not with their feelings running riot and
their minds in turmoil. What would they say to each other?
What would they talk about?

Liza jangled a key chain on her index finger. "Want to do
the honors, darling?" she asked her husband coquettishly.

Chris smiled back as she tossed him the keys. "Since you consider this our first real home, does that mean I'm supposed to carry you over the threshold?"

Liza grinned, pecking him on the cheek. "With your back? I wouldn't think of it, dear. Anyway, I thought you and Emily could go in and get things organized for our picnic while David and I run down to the take-out place for those mouthwatering ribs."

So much for being subtle, Emily thought ruefully. It was as plain as that tight-fitting Lycra number on Liza's body. Chris's wife was making a play for her boyfriend.

Emily shot David a look, thinking he must be in seventh heaven with all this attention being heaped on him by the love of his life. Even if he was trying his damnedest not to show it. Just as she was trying her best not to show that it bothered her. If this was what David wanted . . . If! Ha!

Chris slung an arm round Emily's shoulder in what she took to be a defensive maneuver against his wife's overtly flirtatious behavior toward David.

"Good idea," he said jocularly. "We'll case the place for roaches. At least I can count on Em not to collapse into a dead heap on the floor if we discover any."

"I didn't—" Liza started to protest, but then changed her mind midsentence, snapping up David's hand. "Come on. Let's go." Tugging him over to the car, she called out, "Don't worry if we're a bit late getting back. There are usually big lineups."

David cast a look back at Emily as he got to the car. She was already heading into the house with Chris. They were arm in arm. How cozy, he thought as he watched them with an outlaw glint in his eye. Until Liza's laugh made him look across the car at her.

"You two are an item, aren't you?" Liza's question was purely rhetorical. Which was just as well, since, at that moment, David wasn't sure of the answer.

Emily didn't look back as she heard David's car pull out of the driveway, but she could feel something tighten inside her.

Once inside the villa, Emily obediently joined Chris in an exploration of the house, which was as lovely inside as the outside suggested. The great room—a combination living room/family room—had warm terra-cotta tiled floors, dramatic expanses of window overlooking the sea, curved butter-cream leather couches, and a huge adobe fireplace. The kitchen was off the great room to the east along with a small but attractive rosewood-paneled den. The sleeping area was to the west of the main room—two spacious guest rooms with their own private baths, and a huge master suite that looked like something out of *Architectural Digest.*

The master suite was their last stop on the house tour. Emily stood awkwardly at the open doorway while Chris stepped inside.

"Terrific," he said, heading straight over to the grouping of expensive leather suitcases in one corner of the vast room. "Our stuff actually got here."

As he made his way over to the luggage, he slipped off his sport jacket, tossing it haphazardly onto the king-size bed. When he started to slip the dark blue T-shirt he was wearing under the jacket over his head, Emily quickly averted her gaze. Admittedly, it wasn't easy. From the brief glimpse she'd allowed herself of Chris's bare upper torso, she could see that he'd spent some of his time in New York at a gym. And a tanning salon.

"I'll go and get some plates and stuff together," she mumbled and started to step away.

Bare-chested, one arm hoisting up a case so that his biceps bulged, he called out, "No, don't go off yet, Em. I want to talk to you. We have so much to catch up on."

"I'll be in the kitchen. You can come in after...you're ready."

Chris gave her an amused look. "Come on, Em. I'm just gonna change my shirt. You can handle that, can't you?"

Actually, Emily wasn't so sure. Nor was she so sure about what was going on. Was Chris being deliberately seductive? Oh, she knew being seductive was as natural to him as breathing—when it came to most women. But not her. Never her. Until now.

Emily was in a quandary. There was no way to deny she felt flattered by Chris's sudden attentiveness. There was also no way to deny that he looked tantalizingly alluring standing bare-chested in this lavish and romantic bedroom. She reminded herself that Chris was a married man, and she didn't feature herself as "the other woman." And then there was David to think about.

Yes, David—the man with whom she'd spent some glorious moments of passion. The man whom she viewed as both a lover and a friend. A man she could confide in. A man who was warm, funny, sensitive, talented, and great in bed.

A man who was now off with the woman he'd been in love with practically his whole life. Did Liza really expect her to believe their delay was supposed to have something to do with a long line at the ribs counter? How gullible did Liza think she was? This very minute, the pair were probably parked on a bluff overlooking the ocean, having themselves a ball "catching up on old times."

If Chris was bothered by what his wife and David might at this very moment be doing, he showed no sign of it. He looked remarkably unconcerned as he unzipped the suitcase he'd hoisted onto a low bureau. He flipped open the lid and pulled out two jerseys, one solid red, the other cocoa with white stripes. He held them both up in Emily's direction.

"What do you prefer?" he asked, crossing the room and drawing closer to her.

Emily was forced to lift her gaze from the woven Navaho rug at her feet. Her eyes flitted from one shirt to the other, en route being forced to take in Chris's provocative smile and his broad, muscled, golden chest. He looked like every woman's fantasy. Certainly hers.

What did she prefer? What a question!

"ARE YOU SURE YOU remember the place being down this road?" David asked Liza who, despite the car's bucket seats, had managed to get close enough to him for their thighs to touch.

"You know how awful I am about directions. Maybe we should have gone right at that last fork."

"I'll turn around."

"Then again, maybe it's up ahead a mile or two. This scenery does look familiar."

David cast her a bemused look. All the scenery around there looked pretty much the same.

"Oh, David, a lookout point. Let's pull over. I need to stretch my legs after sitting so long on that cramped plane."

David compressed his lips. Finally, a chance to be alone with Liza at a lookout point—compensation in spades for that awful night of the senior prom when he'd ended up chauffeuring Liza and her boyfriend to a similar spot. The only problem was, David had the feeling he was still going along for the ride. Maybe there wasn't a boyfriend in the back seat with Liza this time. There was, however, a husband back at home. At home alone with Emily. What were the two of them doing? The possibilities proved too disturbing to contemplate.

"Please, David," Liza pleaded sweetly. "Just for a couple of minutes."

After a moment's hesitation, he pulled off into the deserted parking area. Liza leaned forward and switched off the ignition. Instead of getting out of the car and stretching her legs as David expected, she dropped her head on his shoulder, snuggling closer against him.

"Talk to me, David. I always did love the sound of your voice," she murmured in that sultry tone he'd heretofore only heard her use with other men. As if to drive her message home, her hand dropped provocatively onto his thigh.

David was speechless. Even if he could have spoken at that moment, what would he say? Liza was coming on to him. How long had he waited for this moment? His luck, it would come just when he'd all but convinced himself he was over her. Not to mention that Liza was married. As much as he disliked Chris, he had absolutely no desire to cuckold him. And then there was Emily. Emily with her disarming smile, her openness, her gutsiness, her luscious body. Emily, beaming brightly as she went strolling arm in arm with Chris into that empty house, he reminded himself. How were *they* passing the time?

Liza lifted her head, her face so close to his that if he puckered his lips they would have touched hers. "You've always been there for me in the past, David. You're not going to let me down now, are you?"

David stared at her, awash with ambivalence.

10

IT WAS NEARLY TEN o'clock when Emily and David started back for the city. And then, not until after Chris and Liza had wheedled a promise out of them to come back for dinner the following Saturday evening.

"At least I get to sit up front this time," Emily deadpanned as they pulled out of the drive.

David didn't smile. She hadn't thought he would.

"I guess that rib place must have been real busy," she commented idly. There was nothing idle about it, in truth—David and Liza had been gone to pick up those ribs for well over an hour.

"We stopped and talked for a while. Liza's . . . unhappy," David said quietly.

"So is Chris."

They exchanged glances.

"Liza says Chris is totally self-absorbed and snide."

"Chris says Liza's utterly selfish and narcissistic."

There was a strained silence. They didn't speak again until they were on the freeway.

"I told Liza we were seeing each other," David said, his tone almost portentous.

Emily laughed. It came out harsher than she meant it to. "Sorry. It's just the term. *Seeing each other.* It's so . . . tasteful."

"What did you tell Chris about us? Or did you tell him anything?" David demanded angrily.

To Emily the assault of his words was like a slap in the face. Tears came to her eyes. She felt like pieces of herself were breaking off. "I told him we were lovers," she said so quietly, David had to strain to hear.

David's anger immediately turned to chagrin. "Emily..."

She raised her hand to silence him. "No. Don't say anything."

He didn't. For a few minutes. "A short time ago we both felt that we could say anything to each other." His voice was laced with sadness.

Emily bit her lip. "Oh, David. I'm so ... confused."

He took one hand from the steering wheel and reached for hers. "That makes two of us." They clasped each other's hands as though they were both drowning.

"I'm not going to lie to you, David. I still feel...something for Chris. I can't put words to the feelings, but I can't deny they exist. And you still feel ... something for Liza, don't you?"

"Yes," David said simply.

"And she feels something for you," Emily added in a whisper.

"She's confused. She's hurt. She's frightened."

"Chris, too."

"He certainly seemed glad to see you." Resentment and jealousy crept into David's voice.

Emily was too caught up in her own confusion to pick it up. "He's never been this glad to see me before. I don't fully understand it."

"Why don't you? You're a very attractive, desirable woman, Emily."

Any other time, she would have been touched by David's compliment and responded with a warm, grateful thanks.

This wasn't any other time, though. "It's certainly taken Chris long enough to notice."

"If I were just your friend, I'd say better late than never. I'm not just your friend, Emily."

It was one of those moments when everything seemed to stop, like a piece of film jamming in a movie projector.

"I know," Emily said, feeling an awful ache inside.

"So where does that leave us?"

She didn't answer right away. "I'm not sure."

David knew that was going to be her answer. He felt her uncertainty and confusion as much as he felt his own. As much as he knew she felt his.

She closed her eyes and leaned her head against the head-rest.

"Do you think they're going to break up?" she asked finally.

David's hand tightened on the wheel. "I suggested to Liza they go for marital counseling."

Emily smiled. "I told Chris the same thing."

"Emily?"

"Yes, David."

"I'm crazy about you."

Tears escaped her eyes. She'd waited so many weeks to hear him say those words. Only now she couldn't fully embrace them as she'd dreamed of doing. They weren't enough. She knew it and she knew that David knew it. He couldn't be crazy about her and still be a little bit in love with Liza. Any more than she could be crazy about him and still be a little bit in love with Chris. There'd always be doubts, insecurities, fears creeping into their relationship.

What if Chris and Liza split up? What if the objects of their romantic fantasies were once again *available?* Despite Chris's seductive manner toward her that evening, Emily felt sure it had more to do with getting back at his wife than with any shift in his feelings for her. He was jealous of Liza's overt attraction to David—an attraction that Emily saw as genuine. Chris had turned to her because his male ego was under attack and in need of stroking. If he was back on the market, Emily was sure Chris would waste no time finding himself another sexy, glamorous, cover-girl beauty as a replacement for Liza, and she'd go back to being Good Old Em. Funny, but the idea of that didn't really bother Emily as much as it might have. Not as much as it had, certainly, when he'd married Liza. Maybe she felt less for Chris than she'd thought.

Emily only wished the same would turn out to be true for David, but she wasn't going to hold her breath on that wish. All her old insecurities and self-doubts bubbled to the surface. What kind of chance did she stand against Liza, especially when the sultry siren set her sights on a man? What man could resist the dazzling, breathtakingly beautiful Liza? Certainly not one who'd yearned for her practically his whole life.

Emily was shaken from her upsetting ruminations by the car's abrupt stop. She looked out the window. They were in front of David's loft.

David's hand fell lightly on her shoulder. "Spend the night with me, Emily."

Keeping her face averted, she shook her head. Her response didn't come as a surprise to him. He wasn't even sure whether he'd asked her out of love, need, companionship, fear or guilt. He only knew that he felt this awful lump in his throat that wouldn't dissolve.

"Then come up for a little while," he coaxed. "We'll have a glass of wine and listen to some jazz."

"I can't, David. Not . . . tonight."

"We'll talk, Emily. We need to talk."

"No. We need to . . . think."

They sat there with the car idling for a few more minutes in silence, then David pulled out without another word, knowing Emily was right. Knowing didn't make him feel any better, though. He felt miserable. He even found himself wishing Liza had never come back—an admission that took him quite by surprise. What was he feeling for Liza? All those years stumbling over himself to get her to notice him, to care about him, to be attracted to him. Had her sudden shower of attention merely been an answer to old dreams that had worn thin?

When David drew up to Emily's building, she reached for the door handle, desperate for some breathing space. Some crying space. David wasn't going to let her off so easily. With a fierceness that was completely unlike him, he pulled her roughly to him, wrenching her hand from the handle, and ravaged her lips more than kissed them.

Emily's first reaction to David's uncharacteristic ferocity was shock and anger. She intended not to respond at all to his savagery. Within moments, she found herself responding in equal measure. She couldn't help herself. She was feeling as savage as he was.

They broke apart at the same time, their tumultuous emotions too acute to bear. Emily sprang from the car. This time David made no attempt to stop her. Shaken, he watched her race for the lobby of her building, muttering, "Damn, damn, damn," under his breath.

TWO DAYS AFTER STARTING work at *Newsline*, Emily was busy at her desk attacking a pile of back copies of the publication. Bagley wanted her to immerse herself in the "*Newsline* heartbeat," as he put it. She was finishing up with one magazine and about to grab up the next in the stack when a figure flitted by the glass enclosure that separated her cubicle of an office from the corridor.

Emily's hand froze midmotion. It was Liza. No detective work was needed to uncover where she was heading. David's office was two doors past hers.

She checked her watch. Nearly twelve. She and David had talked about having lunch together that afternoon. They were both making an effort to be civilized about all this. After all, they were both floating in the same rudderless boat. With Liza's arrival, Emily had a sinking feeling that she'd be lunching alone.

Five minutes passed and David appeared at her door. Emily looked up at him, her expression blank. Wearing her feelings on her sleeve was becoming too painful. David was wearing one of his awkward smiles. She almost felt sorry for him.

"Hi," she said innocently. "Ready for lunch?" Why make it easy for him? Okay, so she wasn't feeling *that* sorry for him.

David checked his watch even though he knew precisely what time it was. Time was running out. "Yes. Ready." There was a pregnant pause. "Mind if Liza joins us? She was in the neighborhood and...dropped by, thinking we could all have lunch together."

Emily just bet Liza had included her. "On second thought, I promised myself I'd get through five magazines before the day's over and I'm falling behind schedule."

David felt a flash of irritation. He never had cottoned to deceit, but it was especially painful to see it coming from Emily. "I didn't invite her. She just showed up."

She grabbed a magazine and flipped it open. "It's all right, David. Have a nice lunch. Give Liza my best."

"You're being childish, Emily."

Her gaze darted up to his face, the churlishness slipping from her own. "I know," she admitted. "Give me a break, David. I can't do it. I've spent too many years feeling like a fifth wheel."

Her honesty, though appreciated, proved as disturbing as her deceit. "Emily. . ."

Before David could say anything more, Liza came up behind him and grabbed his arm. "I know exactly what I want."

Emily bet she did.

"Thai food."

Emily hated Thai cuisine, and what's more, she knew the same was true for David. He didn't make a peep of protest, however. That, more than anything, put her in a terrible funk for the rest of the day.

THAT NIGHT AFTER WORK, Emily had plans to meet Cheryl for a drink at a popular upscale watering hole halfway between their two offices. When Emily arrived at the trendy hot spot, Cheryl was already there, and had managed to nab a table in a nook away from the hordes of blue suits at the bar.

"You look terrible," Cheryl said without preamble as Emily slid into her seat.

"That'll do wonders for my already shattered ego," she muttered dryly.

"Let me guess. Could it be . . . Liza?" The question, as they both knew, was purely rhetorical.

"She happened to be in the neighborhood at lunchtime and stopped by to see if David wanted to take her to lunch." Emily's tone reeked of sarcasm.

"He accepted, naturally."

"Name me one man who ever turned Liza down for anything."

Cheryl flushed. Emily apologized, remembering that once upon a time Alan Freese, the love of Cheryl's life, had been one of those men. "I guess I put my foot in my mouth," Emily said.

Cheryl smiled. "It's okay. I'm learning to have more self-confidence."

"What's your secret?"

"When I figure it out, you'll be the first one I tell. So, back to lunch. Didn't you tell me on the phone last night that you and David . . . ?"

"Oh, he invited me to join them, pretending that they both wanted me along."

"You said no?"

"I have some pride." Emily scowled. "Besides, I would have gotten sick if I'd had to sit there at a Thai restaurant watching Liza fawn all over David. That wouldn't be the worst part, though. The worst part would be watching David sitting there pretending that he wasn't loving every minute of it. My only consolation is that he's going to have wicked indigestion tonight."

"I can't believe David doesn't see through her," Cheryl said. "She's using him to make Chris jealous. She doesn't care about him."

"Maybe she doesn't. Maybe she does. This is about what David feels."

Cheryl managed to catch an overworked waiter's eye. When he came over, she ordered their usual wine spritzers.

"No," Emily said to the waiter as he started to hurry off. "Make that one wine spritzer, one martini."

Cheryl squinted at her. "Martini? Since when did you start to drink hard liquor?"

"Since today," Emily said resolutely, calling out to the departing waiter to make it a double.

"What about Chris?" Cheryl asked after the drinks arrived. "Have you heard from him?"

"Twice," Emily said with a bemused smile. "He didn't even have a favor to ask of me either time. This is something of a record," she added, taking a large swallow of her drink, which was followed by a fit of coughing.

"Go easy on that stuff. It's potent."

"That's the point," Emily said dryly.

"So, what did he say?" Cheryl prodded.

Emily took another sip of her martini. This swallow went down more easily. "He said that he loved his new job at the studio and if I wanted to come over some time he'd show me around."

Cheryl's eyes widened. "What did you say?"

"I left it open-ended."

"Anything else?"

Emily set down her glass. "He and Liza are discussing marital counseling, but he doesn't know if it will help. He also practically begged me not to back out of this dinner over at their house Saturday night, which I had every intention of backing out of. He insisted he needs me there for moral support." She lifted the glass back to her lips. "It's nice to be needed by someone."

"A while back, you wouldn't have considered Chris just 'someone.'"

Emily sighed. "That's true. I would have been dancing in the streets, throwing confetti. Along with my mother." Emily stared into her drink. "The only thing that would make my mother happier than Chris and I ending up as a twosome is her getting back together with my father. Now you know where I got my wishful thinking from."

"What if it isn't wishful thinking?" Cheryl queried.

Emily swatted away the question with her hand. "It was only two dumb phone calls. He didn't show up at *Newsline* to whisk me off for Thai food."

"You hate Thai food."

"That's beside the point," Emily said, disgruntled, moving the glass to her lips.

Cheryl intercepted her. "Before you get completely pie-eyed, there's something I've got to tell you."

Emily picked up the shift in the timbre of her friend's voice. She gave Cheryl a closer look, noticing for the first time how much trimmer she was looking, and that her complexion seemed creamier, her eyes brighter. In short, Cheryl looked radiant. Emily felt guilty for having been so caught up in her own problems not to have noticed before. It wasn't hard to figure out the reason for the transformation.

"Is it about you and Alan?"

Cheryl broke out in a wide smile. "We're getting married. In two months. I've always wanted a June wedding."

Emily clasped her friend's hand. "Oh, Cheryl, that's wonderful."

"Of course, you're going to be my maid of honor."

Emily smiled wistfully. Always the bridesmaid, never the bride.

"I'd never speak to you again if I wasn't," she said aloud. "I'm so happy for you, Cheryl. I really am. Here I've been going on and on about all this dumb stuff and . . ."

"It's not dumb stuff," Cheryl broke in. "Nothing dumb about it."

Emily sniffed into her damp cocktail napkin. "I think I need another drink."

"You haven't finished your first one."

"You're right. I hate martinis."

THAT SATURDAY EVENING, Emily was stepping out of the shower when the phone rang. It was David.

"Will you be ready in half an hour?" he asked.

She knew she could be ready in ten minutes. "I'm running way behind," she lied. "Why don't you go on ahead and tell them I'll be along as soon as I can."

"It's silly to take two cars. I can wait."

"No, really. I don't mind driving."

Emily would have begged off the dinner altogether if she hadn't promised Chris she would be there. At least now, she wouldn't have to go through the torture of the long ride down there and back alone with David. Ever since their disrupted lunch date, she'd made up her mind to give their relationship plenty of breathing space, afraid the closeness would knock the wind right out of her.

"Okay," David said quietly. "If that's the way you want it."

"Yes. It's the way I want it," Emily replied, disappointed that he'd given in so easily.

WHEN EMILY ARRIVED AT the villa in Newport Beach, the door was ajar so she let herself in and crossed the foyer into the great room. When she got to the arched entryway, she came to an abrupt halt, a gasp choking in her throat. It was almost déjà vu, save for the fact that this time it wasn't Chris whom Emily discovered entwined in Liza's arms on the sofa. This time it was David.

Emily turned to flee, afraid she was going to be sick right on those spotless terra-cotta tiles. Her escape wasn't successful.

"Emily!" David cried out.

She kept going. He caught up to her as she got to the door. "It's not what you're thinking, Emily."

She shook off his touch. "I see you and Liza decided to start 'dining' without me. Or Chris."

"Chris left."

"How obliging of him."

David spun her around. "He walked out on Liza. They had a big fight and he stormed out just as I pulled into the drive. Liza was crying hysterically. I was only comforting her."

"And doing a very good job of it."

"Come on, Emily. She's devastated. They're going to split up. She thinks Chris has been having an affair."

She gave him an accusatory look. "Are you sure the shoe shouldn't be on the other foot?"

David stared at her, dumbstruck. Emily wasn't only accusing Liza of being the one having the affair, she was accusing her of having it with him.

"I'm sorry," Emily said haltingly. She'd only made the accusation to hurt him because she was hurting so much. She knew that David wasn't the kind of man who would sleep with a married woman, even if he'd wanted to; even if that married woman was Liza. Only it didn't look like Liza was going to be married much longer....

As they stood there, with Liza's muted sobs drifting in from the other room, David and Emily could see their relationship disintegrating right before their eyes. They both wanted to stop it, but neither of them knew how.

"David," Liza called out, her voice husky from crying.

Emily's muscles tightened. "You'd better go to her. She needs you." Wasn't this what he'd always dreamed about? And now that Liza and Chris were splitting up, what was there to stop David from realizing his dream?

"We could both—" David began.

"I wouldn't be very good at doling out sympathy just now," she said, cutting him off and fleeing out the door.

EMILY WAS A WRECK when she finally got home. All she wanted to do was crawl into bed and try to forget that David, Chris or Liza had ever existed. Not a likely prospect, especially when she discovered Chris sitting on the floor outside her front door.

He scrambled to his feet as she approached and gave her a winsome, heartfelt smile. "I was hoping you wouldn't stay there too late."

Emily stared at him. "How did you get into the building?"

His smile turned a bit smug. "One of the pluses of being a celebrity. A neighbor recognized me."

Emily stood there, key ring dangling on her finger. Chris took the key ring from her, opening her door. "Can I come in for a while, Em? There's really no one else I feel close enough to confide in."

Emily's heart was racing. Was she hearing right? Chris felt close to her. He'd certainly kept it a well-guarded secret up to now.

She gestured for him to come in, not trusting her voice. No sooner had he stepped inside and closed the door behind him than he pulled a stunned Emily into his arms.

"Oh, Em, I feel so alone, so misunderstood, so lost," he murmured into her hair. "Let me hold you for a minute, Em. I need to feel . . . connected."

Emily felt completely *dis*connected. It was as if her whole world had just done a complete flip. She was suddenly hanging from her toes, the blood rushing to her head. "Chris . . ."

He pressed his cheek against hers, stroking her back. "It was the worst mistake of my life, marrying Liza. A mistake I intend to rectify as soon as possible. Liza never was sensitive to my needs, never took the time to understand me, never gave me the kind of respect I deserved. Being a sportscaster is a lot more than reading copy off a TelePrompTer. It takes a special talent, Em. The work is very intense, very demanding, very draining. Did Liza ever see that? Was she the least bit supportive? Was it any wonder I...strayed once or twice?"

Emily stiffened. *Strayed?* So, Liza was right. Chris had cheated on her.

He held her tighter. "Don't think I haven't been racked with guilt, Em. I'm a one-woman man. You know that. I just want to make a clean break and start all over. You can understand what I'm saying, can't you, Em?"

Emily wasn't sure she understood anything at this point, but she nodded her head, not knowing what else to do.

Still holding her, he edged his head away and bathed her in his killer smile. "I knew I could count on you, Em. You've always been so giving, so generous, so nurturing, so undemanding."

He stroked her cheek. "Have I been blind all these years, or have you suddenly turned beautiful, Em?"

Emily blushed.

"You *are* beautiful, Em. Beautiful, soft, sensitive, loving. I need that, Em. You don't know how much I need a woman who can really be there for me. Be there for me now, Em." As he crooned, he nuzzled her neck, his hands sliding sinuously down her spine.

Emily couldn't believe what was happening. Chris was propositioning her.

Okay, she told herself, *he isn't perfect. He can be a little self-absorbed, insensitive, oblivious. On the plus side, he's charming, gorgeous, dripping with sexual magnetism, and I've dreamed about this moment practically my whole life.*

She thought about David; about the friendship and passion they'd shared; about her growing and deepening feelings for him—feelings she'd thought were mutual.

Suddenly, she flashed on David and Liza wrapped in each other's arms, not seeing them clothed on the couch now, but naked on that enormous bed in that romantic master bedroom. . . .

Chris guided her over to her couch, drew her down on his lap. He was doing his best to try to seduce her. If she was going to be honest with herself, Emily would have admitted that it was more anger and betrayal about what she imagined was going on in that villa in Newport Beach than desire for Chris that made her try to get in the mood and enjoy this moment she'd awaited for so long—a moment she'd never truly believed would ever happen. How ironic that now that it was happening, she found herself feeling that something was missing. Something inside her. Something called her *heart*, which she'd once again gone and foolishly deposited in another unattainable man's lap.

She pried herself off Chris's lap and stood. "We can't do this."

He tried to draw her back down, but she resisted. "I can't. You need time to sort things out, Chris. And so do I. You'd better go."

He rose reluctantly from the sofa, curving his arms lightly around her neck. "You don't really want me to go, Em. You couldn't." He looked as incredulous at being rebuffed as she felt rebuffing an offer she'd never dreamed she would refuse.

"I'm sorry, Chris. Please try to understand—"

"If you're thinking this is a one-night stand, or that all I'm looking for is the mere comfort of a willing body, or that I don't feel like sleeping alone in some hotel suite, you're wrong, Em. I'm seeing you for the first time. My eyes are open now."

Unfortunately, so were Emily's. She, too, was seeing Chris for the first time.

"I'm flattered, Chris, but I think you should leave."

He looked about to argue, but then he produced another of his killer smiles, pecked her cheek, then ambled toward her door. "It's been a long time since I was turned down, Em." He opened the door. "I'll tell you the truth. I never thought you'd be the one to do it. It just goes to show you."

To Emily's astonishment, Chris sounded more awed than dejected.

He gave her a foxy wink and exited.

DAVID WENT TO HAND LIZA the mug of tea he'd made for her, but she waved it off. He set it down on the coffee table.

"I must look a sight."

David smiled distractedly, still disturbed by Emily's flight from the house. "You look fine."

"My head is splitting."

"Want me to get you a couple of aspirin?"

Liza shook her head, patting the cushion beside her on the couch. David hesitated for a moment, then sat down.

She snuggled against him. "I don't know what I ever saw in Chris, I honestly don't. He's so shallow, so vain, so oblivious to my needs." She looked up at David, her violet eyes wide and glistening, and not a hint of red even after all her crying. "I have needs, David. I may look superconfident, but I'm really very insecure, very vulnerable."

She spread her palm across his chest. Could she feel his heart racing? "I have to be stroked, David. I have to be reassured. I have to be treated with kid gloves."

Her other hand slid around his neck. "Chris accused me of being spoiled and pampered. He said it as if he were charging me with a crime. You tell me, David. If a man truly loves a woman, shouldn't he want to spoil her? And pamper her?" Her ruby lips were inches from his. "Wouldn't *you*, David?"

She was offering him those divine lips. All he had to do was lean his head forward and claim them. Never had a few inches felt like such a vast distance. He couldn't do it. More amazing, he didn't *want* to. He'd sat here for close to two hours listening to Liza drone on and on about how Chris had failed her as a husband. What he was really hearing—hearing for the first time—was how needy, dependent and demanding Liza was.

Again, he found himself making comparisons between Liza and Emily. And then it struck him. The crux of the difference between the two women was that with Emily it would never be a one-way street. Emily knew how to give as well as receive. Emily was honest, generous, funny, intelligent. She had depth and character. How could he have let her run off like he had?

He sprang up from the couch as Liza was closing the gap between their lips. She nearly fell, face forward, into the cushions.

"I have to go, Liza." He could hear the desperation in his own voice.

Liza was oblivious. She reached up and pulled him back down. "You can't leave me, David. I'm so miserable, so lonely, so . . . desperate. You, of all people, wouldn't desert me in my time of need."

"I'm not deserting you, Liza. I'm going home. We both need a good night's sleep. Things will look a whole lot clearer in the morning."

She gripped a handful of his shirt. "They're clear right now, David. I'm finally seeing everything as clear as glass."

He pried her fingers from the fabric and stood again. "I'd be taking advantage of you if I stayed," he lied—badly. "You're at a very vulnerable time now, Liza."

"Oh, David, that's just like you. You've always been so caring, so considerate, so sensitive," she murmured, circling her arms around him. "You wouldn't be taking advantage of me, though. One thing you know is true about me. I've always known what I wanted. I know what I want now, David. I knew it as soon as I saw you at the airport last week."

As David felt Liza's body press against his, he told himself he must be going out of his mind. Was he really going to turn down an offer of a lifetime? Here was his chance to finally make love to the woman of his dreams.

That was the problem. In his *dreams*, Liza had always been everything he'd ever wanted—or *thought* he wanted. Real life was another story altogether.

He gave her a light peck on the cheek. "I'll give you a call in the morning."

Liza grabbed hold of his arm as he started to leave. "I want you to know, David, even if Chris should show up tonight and get down on his knees and beg me to forgive him and take him back, I won't. It's over between us, David. I want to start fresh. I see things so clearly now."

David nodded and made a hasty retreat. He, too, was seeing things clearly now.

EMILY WAS DOZING OFF when her downstairs buzzer jarred her from sleep. She groggily glanced at her clock radio. It was after eleven. She threw off her covers and shuffled down the hall to the intercom.

"Who is it?"

"Emily, it's me, David. I've got to talk to you."

Emily could hear the angst and desperation in his voice as she stared at the speaker on her wall. He probably wanted to come upstairs to confess he was still in love with Liza and break things off cleanly with her. Honestly. Emily, however, had had all the "honesty" she could handle for one day. And all the men.

"It's late, David. I was already in bed. I'm exhausted."

"Emily . . ."

"I'll see you at work on Monday." She was going to take Sunday off to recuperate. Fat chance! "Good night, David."

She clicked off. David buzzed her one more time. Emily shook her head wearily and shuffled off back to bed. Exhausted as she was, she held out little hope of falling asleep now.

Standing in the entryway to the building, David squinted at the intercom. "Okay, Emily. I get it. You want me to suffer a little for staying to comfort Liza. Let me tell you, Emily, listening to Liza whine for over two hours was suffering enough for any man. That's part of what I came to tell you, Emily. The rest . . ." He shook his head and turned away, smiling. "The rest I'll tell you when you're listening to me. Good night, Emily Bauer. Sleep tight. I love you."

CHRIS ANDERS ARRIVED ON Emily's doorstep at nine o'clock the next morning, Sunday paper in one hand, and a bag full of coffee and croissants in the other. Emily, only half-awake, stared at him with a befuddled look.

He grinned. "I met another of your neighbors outside. A real sports fan. I had to give her an autograph for her mom, as well. I think it's great that more women are getting into sports shows these days. Mine anyway," he said cockily.

"Chris, what are you doing here?"

"Bringing you breakfast. It's about time, don't you think?" She stared at him groggily.

"All those times you showed up at my door with special treats." He stepped into her apartment. "Em, Em, what a jerk

I was. There I was, thinking the grass was always greener. Well, your lawn looks terrific, Em."

As his eyes did a slow cruise up and down her body, it dawned on Emily that she was standing there in an old, worn terry robe, her hair uncombed, her teeth not even brushed. Her hand went to her mouth. "I've got to go . . . wash up."

"Go ahead, sweetheart. I'll have breakfast ready for you in a jiffy."

Sweetheart. Emily could only shake her head in amazement. The phone rang as she was about to step into the bathroom. Chris picked it up like he was living there.

"Hi, Mrs. Bauer," he said cheerfully.

He winked at Emily, shooing her off, but she stood there listening—and cringing at what her mother was going to make of Chris answering her phone at nine in the morning.

"No, it's not David. It's Chris. . . . That's right, Chris Anders. . . . No, I'm alone. Just me and Em . . . What am I doing here? Seeing to it that your daughter eats a nice, hearty breakfast. That's what I'm doing here."

Emily rolled her eyes. Her mother would never let her hear the end of this. She was probably, right this very minute, thumbing through the Yellow Pages under Wedding Coordinators.

"Oh, I will, Mrs. Bauer. . . . Okay. Naomi . . . That's a promise."

Emily folded her arms across her chest as he hung up. "What did you promise?"

He sauntered over to her. "I promised her we'd have a lovely morning. I always keep my promises." He bent down to plant a kiss on her lips.

Emily quickly averted her face. "Morning breath," she mumbled.

He settled for a bear hug that pinned Emily's arms to her side. "You're great, Em. Always sensitive to the other guy. That's why I'm nuts about you."

When he released her, Emily gave him a wilted smile. He was nuts about her and that was all she could muster. A wilted smile. She was in a bad way.

"I'm going to brush my teeth," she muttered, retreating to the bathroom.

Her timing couldn't have been worse. While she was in the bathroom, her downstairs buzzer rang. The water was running so she didn't hear it. She did, however, hear her doorbell chime a minute later and popped her head out of the bathroom just as Chris was opening the door.

"Oh, I thought you were the florist," Chris said blandly.

David, who was standing on the other side of the door, didn't say a word. He stared from Chris to Emily in her robe at her bathroom door, putting the wrong two-and-two together. Then he spun around and took off.

Emily closed her eyes and sagged against the wall. Chris turned to her with a sheepish smile. "Hey, you don't think he thought . . ."

"It doesn't matter." *Let him think we both ended up getting what we wanted.*

"YOU DON'T LOOK VERY happy to see me, David."

"Yes, I am. It's just that I wasn't expecting you."

"Aren't you going to ask me in?"

David stepped away from his door as Liza swept inside. She was wearing a skintight black Lycra sheath, and she looked sensational. *Her husband walks out on her, she gets a good night's sleep, and he spends the night tossing and turning. There was no justice in this world.*

"I always did love this place. Not that it couldn't use a woman's touch." She spun around to face him. "You know the biggest mistake I made?"

"What?"

"Moving out of here and into Emily's apartment. If I'd stayed put I never would have met Chris. More than that," she murmured, approaching him, "I might have realized that you were the man for me all along." When she got to him, her hands slithered around his neck.

Even though David was convinced Chris had spent the night with Emily and that was the real reason she hadn't let him come up the night before, he wasn't capable of playing tit for tat. Besides, he was sure Liza was coming on to him so fiercely simply to mask her upset over the split.

He did have to admit it was disconcerting to see just how well she masked it. Wouldn't it be crazy if she really were to fall in love with him? At one time the thought of that happening would have filled him with pure elation. Now, he was amazed to discover he felt nothing but a sinking dread. He took gentle hold of her wrists and drew her arms down to her sides.

"I know you're scared, Liza. I know you feel alone. I know what you're going through."

Her eyes shimmered. "See how well you know me." She tucked her head on his shoulder. "You smell so good, David. Is that the Ralph Lauren cologne I bought you last Christmas?"

As David recalled, the only thing he'd gotten from Liza last Christmas was a card. A rather innocuous one, at that. The cologne was a gift, though. From Emily. She'd bought it for him on a whim a few weeks ago.

"It's not Lauren," David said, deliberately ambiguous. He didn't want to hurt Liza's feelings. It wasn't her fault that she was so oblivious and self-centered; it was his fault for having spent most of his life overlooking it.

"I have a wonderful day planned for us," she said brightly, managing to free her wrists from his hold and slide her arms around his waist. "We'll start with breakfast omelets at the Sidewalk Café in Venice—"

"I don't eat omelets. I try to stay away from eggs—"

"After breakfast, we'll rent roller blades and skate along the boardwalk—"

"I've never even tried regular roller skates—"

"After that we'll go to this new spa for shiatsu massages."

"Shi— What?"

"Shiatsu. Surely you've had a shiatsu massage before?"

David shook his head. Not only hadn't he had one, he wasn't at all eager to have the experience.

"You'll love it, David. There's simply nothing better in this world—" Liza stopped, smiling coyly. "Except for maybe one or two things, but we can include them after we lunch at the Polo Club. It's absolutely *the* place to go to see Hollywood in action."

"Liza, I don't think—"

"You don't want to go to the Polo Club? All right. That's fine. I'm very flexible. Despite what Chris says about me." She frowned. "He didn't come home last night. Not that I'm surprised. How much do you want to bet he didn't spend the night alone?"

Sadly, that was one bet David wouldn't wager a plugged nickel on.

11

"I DON'T REALLY KNOW where to begin. I've never done this sort of thing before...talk to a psychiatrist. Okay, here it is in a nutshell. There's this man, David. He and I were friends. Well, we didn't really start off as friends. That was part of the problem. We solved it, though. Only, of course, in the end we didn't. Am I making any sense? I'm not, am I?"

"I'm sure you will make sense in time. Go on, Miss Bauer."

"Maybe I should start with Chris. Now, Chris and I definitely started off as friends. Well...no, that's not quite true, either. I was his friend, but he wasn't really mine although, believe me, I did everything I could to make him my friend. Not that I really wanted him to be my friend. I really wanted him to be more than a friend. Basically, we never really were friends."

"You and Chris weren't friends, but you and David were friends."

"And then David and I became lovers. There was still Chris and Liza."

"Liza?"

"Haven't I told you about her yet? Liza's the crux of the whole problem. No, that's not fair. Can she help it if every man whose path she crosses wants her? Then again, she does seem to make a habit of crossing over to my path and tripping me up."

"She trips you up?"

"Can I start all over? I think I'm making this more complicated than it is."

"Please."

"It's very simple. Liza is the woman David was in love with practically his whole life. And Chris is the man I was in love with practically my whole life. So, when we ended up in bed that first time—"

"You and Chris."

"No. David and I. After the wedding."

"You and David got married."

"No. Chris and Liza got married."

"You and David slept together after Chris and Liza got married."

"Exactly. It was an unmitigated disaster. We were depressed, more than a little high and well . . . it sort of just happened. To be honest, I wasn't that high. Later, David confessed he wasn't, either. We both admitted—again down the road—that we had a damn good time. Not the next morning, though. The next morning was dreadful. We were both drowning in guilt. Our only hope was that we'd never have to see each other again. Only we kept on meeting at parties, fashion shows, restaurants. At first it was awkward. Then it got to be less awkward. Then we got to be friends."

"So you were lovers, then you were friends."

"Then we were lovers again. Only this time it was different."

"Different?"

"Better. Much better. Definitely much better. Not that we weren't both still very confused about our feelings."

"Your feelings for each other."

"And mine for Chris and his for Liza. Sometimes I do think David must have been more confused than I was. Not right off. Not until Chris and Liza came back to L.A. Then we were both pretty confused. Hell, I think we all were pretty confused. When Chris and Liza separated I got even more confused. David, however, got 'unconfused' fast, once Liza set her sights on him. He was like putty in her hands."

"You sound very angry."

"I am angry. I'm angry, miserable, confused. Is it any wonder I thought it might help to talk things out with a psychotherapist. Actually, this was Cheryl's idea."

"Cheryl?"

"My friend."

"Cheryl *is* your friend."

"Absolutely. . . Well, I haven't been as good a friend lately as I might be. I've been so . . . preoccupied."

"With Chris."

"And David. And Liza. Do you think I could be feeling a little jealous of Cheryl because her love life is so uncomplicated? She loves Alan, he loves her. They're going to get married and live happily ever after."

"Are you telling me you are jealous, Miss Bauer?"

"No. Not jealous. Envious, maybe. And nervous. Very nervous."

"Why is that?"

"Because I'm going to be Cheryl's maid of honor. Her wedding's next Sunday."

"And that makes you nervous."

"No. What makes me nervous is that David is going to be Alan's best man."

"So, you're nervous because you will be seeing David."

"Oh, I see him every day. We work together. It's horrible."

"Working together is horrible."

"Not exactly the working together. I put on a very good front at work. You wouldn't even recognize me, I'm so . . . upbeat. Naturally, David's disgustingly cheerful. Why shouldn't he be? He got what he always wanted and he doesn't even have to feel guilty because he thinks I got what I always wanted, too."

"You don't have what you always wanted?"

"Oh, I have it. Only I don't want it."

"You don't want what?"

"Not what. Who. Chris."

"I see."

"You don't see the half of it. He wants me. All these years dreaming of him wanting me and now he does."

"Chris."

"Yes. He says I'm the greatest thing since whipped cream. Naturally, that's a very flattering thing for a man to say to a woman. Especially when you've lived practically your whole life praying he'd say you were the greatest thing since whipped cream."

"You're flattered."

"I've never really cared all that much for whipped cream."

"But you cared for Chris."

"I longed for him. I worshipped him from afar, all the while convinced that we were meant for each other. I absolutely believed we were. I kept telling myself that someday he would realize that there was no other woman for him but me."

"Which he now realizes."

"Yes. Yes. He wants me. He yearns for me. He sends me flowers, candy. He writes me love poems. He even read a sonnet to me over the air at the close of one of his shows. A few months ago, if this had happened I'd have been in seventh heaven. Now, it all seems so shallow, so…meaningless. I'm not even doing anything to encourage him. Just the opposite. The more I put him off, the more entranced with me he is. He loves that I'm playing hard to get. Only I'm not playing hard to get. I don't want to be gotten. My mother thinks I've gone off my rocker. She can't understand why I'm not floating on cloud nine."

"She doesn't understand how you feel about Chris?"

"She doesn't *want* to understand. My mother can't let go of the past. She's still waiting for my dad to dump his gorgeous young wife and come back to her. She never lets go."

"And you want to let go of the past."

"Yes. Yes, there is no past for me before David. I had this conviction that Chris was meant for me, but it was based purely on fantasy. I never really knew Chris. When I finally got to know him I realized how dumb fantasies can be sometimes. It was different with David. The more I knew him, the better I liked him. We could talk to each other, work with each other, and we could make love like there was no tomorrow. Only tomorrow finally came. Now, David's with Liza...."

"I SUPPOSE I SHOULD HAVE come back sooner. Sometimes I think if I had come back sooner, none of this would have happened. Then again . . ."

"Do you want to share with the group what has happened, David?" John asked.

"Where do I begin? Where did I leave off?"

Bill shot his hand up. "I remember. You were nuts about some gal...."

"Liza, wasn't it?" Grant queried. "Your description of her made me think of Liza Minelli."

"Oh, yeah," Larry interjected. "Liza'd gotten married, you were nursing a broken heart, and then this other gal came along.... Amanda, I think it was."

"Emily. Her name's Emily."

"Right," Larry said. "Emily. I remember now. She was nuts about Liza's husband?"

"She still is," David said, downcast. "I suppose, looking in from the outside, you could say both our dreams came true. We both got what we always wanted. Chris and Liza split up. Now Emily and Chris are going together and Liza is practically throwing herself at me."

Maury studied David. "Sometimes, when dreams come true the truth can be a disappointment."

"It's a nightmare. I'm not in love with Liza. This vision I had of her was based on pure adolescent fantasy. She was this beautiful, desirable, unattainable goddess. I used to think...if I could have her, everything in my life would be perfect and wonderful."

"Now you have her," John observed, "and your life is neither perfect nor wonderful?"

"I'm miserable. You all probably think I'm nuts. Here's this ravishing woman whom I yearned for ever since I was a boy, throwing herself at me, pleading with me to be her lover and—"

"You still haven't slept with her?" Grant broke in incredulously.

"I *can't* sleep with her. I'm not in love with her. I'm in love with Emily." David looked around at the group. "Oh, I know what you're all thinking. That I'm just a guy who always wants what he doesn't have. It isn't like that at all. My feelings for Emily were never based on fantasy. Emily and I were friends as well as lovers. The more we shared, the closer we got. We cared about each other, comforted each other, saw each other at our worst as well as our best. We're even working together now, although I'm thinking about transferring to the magazine's branch office in Seattle. It's pure torture being with Emily, wanting her so desperately, seeing how happy she is with Chris, pretending that I'm just as happy, now that I've finally got Liza. I really blew it with Emily."

"Have you told Emily how you feel?" John asked.

David shook his head. "I can't. What would be the point? She's in love with Chris. She was always in love with him. And he's wooing her like a man obsessed. He sends her a red rose to the office every morning, calls her three, four times a day, picks her up in his zippy red Alfa-Romeo sports car after work, reads love poems to her on his show. I've got to hand it to Emily. She's playing it cool. Letting Chris do the chasing, finally. Making him pursue her. I'm happy for her. It's what she always wanted."

"You don't sound all that happy for her," Maury observed.

David started to protest, then sighed. "Chris isn't the man for Emily."

"How do you know that?" John asked.

He gave the whole group a heartfelt look. "Because Emily was meant for me."

12

IT WAS FUNNY HOW THINGS had come full circle, Emily thought wistfully as she stood in the reception room watching her friend Cheryl dance her first dance with her new husband. Her relationship with David had begun at a wedding and now it was coming to an end at another wedding. That Friday at work, David had told her that he was transferring to *Newsline*'s Seattle offices. She couldn't bring herself to ask him if Liza was going with him. Wishing him good luck was hard enough.

There he was across the ballroom, looking so handsome in his gray cutaway. No doubt about it, he was the best man. And there was Liza, radiant and alluring in a fuchsia satin strapless evening dress, standing beside him, talking animatedly, both arms entwined around his waist as if he were her prize possession. She caught David's eye for an instant, then quickly averted her gaze, letting it shift to Chris. She'd invited him to be her escort for Cheryl's wedding only because she knew that David would be bringing Liza.

"I never thought fuchsia was her color," Chris said snidely. "She only wears colors like that because she wants to make sure she stands out in a crowd."

"She does," Emily said in a monotone.

Chris stroked her arm. "I'm glad I finally have a woman who doesn't."

Emily shot him a look.

"I mean that in the best of ways, Em," he said quickly. "You don't know what it's like always being with a woman who has to be the center of attention or she's not happy. You end up feeling as if you're . . . an accessory."

"I doubt you were ever an accessory," Emily said dryly.

Chris missed the sarcasm. "See, that's why I'm so wild about you, Em. You're always there to pump me up."

The bandleader was asking the guests to join the happy couple on the dance floor.

Chris took her hand. "Shall we?"

Emily started to turn him down until she saw David and Liza heading for the dance floor. She knew this charade was dumb and ridiculous, yet she couldn't bear to have David know how truly miserable she was. One more week and he'd be gone. Would his absence make it any easier? she wondered, as Chris folded her in his arms and began to lead her in a fox-trot. Would it stop the erotic dreams of making love with David that invaded her sleep every night? Would her yearning for her lover, her friend, subside once he was gone? Emily sincerely doubted it.

"Relax, Em. You're so stiff."

"I'm not a very good dancer," she muttered, staring into Chris's shoulder and trying to pretend that she was enjoying herself.

"You need to loosen up a little, that's all. You're not uptight because you're worried about how I'm feeling with Liza being here, are you? If you are, believe me, baby, you're worrying for nothing. I'm over her. She doesn't mean a thing to me. She could get down on her knees in the middle of this dance floor and beg me to come back, and I wouldn't give her the time of day. I'll tell you, I pity David. He doesn't know what he's letting himself in for."

"Doesn't he?" Emily muttered morosely, only to spot David and Liza dancing a few yards away.

David tried to pretend he didn't see them, but Liza gave them both a wide smile as she nudged David in their direction. Chris gripped Emily tighter, swaying her to the music. Liza refused to cooperate with David's efforts to dance past them.

"Lovely wedding, isn't it?" Liza trilled, keeping a firm, proprietary hold on David as she gave Emily's mint-green off-the-shoulder matte jersey gown an appraising look. "Great cut for you, Em. Who was the designer?"

"Beverly Evans," Emily took some small pleasure in telling her, knowing Liza had always envied the success and celebrity of the top L.A. designer.

Liza turned to David who looked as uncomfortable as Emily was sure she looked. "Doesn't Em look nice in that gown, darling?" she cooed.

David gave the gown a quick glance. "Very nice," he mumbled.

Liza smiled acidly at her soon-to-be-ex-husband. "I thought you were going to finally spring for a new tux, Chris."

Chris's features darkened. "This *is* a new tux."

"My mistake," Liza said airily.

"For a fashion designer, you're not terribly observant," Chris snickered, no longer swaying to the music.

"Chris, please," Emily pleaded as some of the guests fox-trotting nearby started staring at them. "Let's dance."

If Chris heard her, he gave no sign of it. He glared at Liza, waiting for the counter-punch. He didn't have to wait long.

"I'm observant enough to notice that you didn't get this tux tailored any better than you did the last one."

"Liza, you don't want to start anything here," David pleaded quietly, putting his hand on her shoulder.

Liza gave him an impatient look. "Am I right or not, David? Look at the way his jacket hangs."

"This tux is perfectly tailored," Chris said acerbically, trailing Liza's gown with a caustic look. "Unlike you, I happen to like having a little room to breathe in my clothes."

"Do you have the gall to imply that this gown is too tight?"

The music stopped in time for most of the couples on the dance floor to catch Liza's angry retort. All eyes turned to them. David and Emily gave each other helpless looks.

Cheryl and Alan came over just as the band was striking up the next tune. Cheryl quickly nabbed Chris for the dance and Alan waltzed off with Liza. It was one way of preserving the peace.

It was also one way of leaving David and Emily alone together in the middle of the dance floor. They stared awkwardly at each other, both of them feeling adrift. David ran a hand down the back of his head. Emily removed some nonexistent strands of hair from her face.

"Would you . . . like to dance?" he asked falteringly.

Emily shook her head. As she started to turn away, David caught hold of her shoulder. The next thing she knew, they were dancing. Emily glanced around the dance floor to see that both Chris and Liza kept darting proprietary glances in their direction even though their new dance partners were doing their best to divert them.

"I don't think Liza likes the idea of our dancing together," Emily murmured.

"I don't think Chris does, either."

Emily swallowed. It was almost more than she could bear to be in David's arms again. He was even wearing the cologne she'd given him. She drew back a little. They smiled politely at each other, all the while their eyes holding memories and emotions they were both trying hard to veil.

"Strange how it all turned out," Emily said softly.

David felt like his heart was being squeezed. Every breath he took hurt. How was he going to make it through the rest of his days without her? "Yes. *Strange* is the word."

Emily was actually relieved when Chris cut in. Liza wasn't far behind to reclaim David.

"I could use some fresh air," Emily said to Chris as the dance ended. "Let's go out onto the terrace."

As it turned out, David had the same need for air. He and Liza were already out on the terrace when Emily and Chris arrived. The instant Emily saw David and Liza standing arm in arm, bathed in moonlight, she was swamped by such a feeling of anguish and loss that she felt as if she would come apart at the seams if she stayed out there another minute.

"I changed my mind. It's . . . too warm. Let's . . . go inside," she said to Chris with an edge of desperation.

Chris gave a distracted nod. "I'll be right in. I want to have one more word with Liza about . . ."

Emily was already dashing inside before she could hear the rest of Chris's sentence. She didn't care what he was saying. Let him make a scene. It didn't matter. Nothing mattered anymore.

She stayed in the ballroom for a few minutes, but the air of happiness and festivity in there proved more than she could tolerate. Tears were streaming down her face by the time she burst into the lobby. She hurried over to a forest-green velvet settee in a secluded alcove and dug in her purse for her handkerchief. Before she could find it, someone was waving a tissue in her face.

"You supplied me with one the last time. Remember?"

Emily looked up, startled to see David standing there. She was even more startled to see that his eyes were watery.

She stood up, her tear-filled eyes fixed on his. The charade was over. They were both wearing their feelings on their sleeves, and all over their faces.

"I thought you and Liza . . ."

He shook his head. "I thought you and Chris . . ."

She shook her head.

"Emily."

"Yes, David?"

"Do you believe that two people can be meant for each other?"

A tremulous smile danced on her lips. "Yes, David. I do."

"I love you, Emily."

"I love you, David."

He was pulling her into his arms when they heard the sound of two familiar squabbling voices entering the lobby from the ballroom.

"I wasn't the one who embarrassed them!" Liza snapped. "If they took off, it's because of you. You never know when to leave well enough alone."

"You started it," Chris retorted. "You deliberately attacked my tailor."

"Oh, shut up. As soon as I find David, we're getting out of here."

"Believe me, Emily and I have had just about enough of your vindictive—"

"Vindictive? I'm vindictive? The nerve . . ."

"Quick, before they spot us," David said, grabbing Emily's hand and whisking her out of the lobby into the street. Laughing, crying, they fell into each other's arms the minute they made their escape, kissing breathlessly, joyously—exactly like two people who were meant to be together.

"Does this mean you won't go to Seattle?" Emily asked, her arms encircling his neck.

David pulled her close again, lifting her off her feet. "I don't know. I hear it's a great place for a honeymoon."

Emily gave him a captivating smile. "There's only one way to find out for sure."

Temptation

Lost Loves

'Right Man...Wrong time'

All women are haunted by a lost love—a disastrous first romance, a brief affair, a marriage that failed.

A second chance with him...could change everything.

Lost Loves, a powerful, sizzling mini-series from Temptation starts in March 1995 with...

The Return of Caine O'Halloran by JoAnn Ross

MILLS & BOON

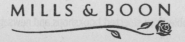

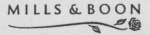

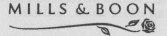

This month's irresistible novels from

Temptation

GETTING RID OF BRADLEY by Jennifer Crusie

Since divorcing Bradley, Lucy hadn't had much luck. Her car had blown up, then her bed! And when sexy cop Zack moved into her house to protect her, he proved to be even more dangerous to her equilibrium!

UNDERCURRENT by Lisa Harris

Fire, Wind, Earth, Water—but nothing is more elemental than passion.

When FBI agent Gus Raphael asked Susannah to help him out, it was the adventure of a lifetime—and her last chance to convince Gus she was everything he wanted. But was his becoming her lover all part of the con?

YOU WERE MEANT FOR ME by Elise Title

Emily loved Chris. David loved Liza. But Chris and Liza loved each other. When Emily and David met at the wedding they found they had a lot in common. But just when did comfort and consolation turn into mutual desire?

LOVE, ME by Tiffany White

Chelsea needed a hit song to save her music career—and sexy songwriter Dakota Law was just the man to write it. But he'd need persuading… Perhaps she could convince him that she could fulfil all his wildest desires…and more.

Spoil yourself next month
with these four novels from

THE PERSONAL TOUCH by Candace Schuler

Lawyer Matt Ryan hadn't anticipated falling for the owner of a
classy dating service. And when rumours started that the
service was a front for criminal activity, he knew that
Susannah could be very dangerous—both for his career and his
heart...

BABY BLUES by Kristine Rolofson

When single mother Anne Winston returned to her home town
with her daughter, she was shocked to learn that sexy Chris
Bogart had moved back, too. He was about to learn that he was
a father. But could they become a family?

THE RETURN OF CAINE O'HALLORAN by JoAnn Ross

Lost Loves mini-series

Ten years ago, Caine and Nora had married because she was
pregnant—but their son's death tore apart their fragile union.
Since then Caine had experienced fame and glory, but now he
wanted more—Nora. Could he win her back?

C.J.'S DEFENCE by Carolyn Andrews

Successful attorney Roarke Farrell was determined to strip
away the sexy little suits opposing attorney C.J. Parker wore in
court—and to tear down the defences around her heart! *And*
he'd knock a hole in her legal defence a mile wide!

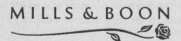

To celebrate 10 years of Temptation we are giving away a host of tempting prizes...

10th All you have to do is complete the wordsearch puzzle below and send it to us by 31 May 1995.

The first 10 correct entries drawn from the bag will each win 12 month's free supply of exciting Temptation books (4 books every month with a total annual value of around £100).

The second 10 correct entries drawn will each win a 200g box of *Thorntons* Temptations chocolates.

I	F	G	N	I	T	I	C	X	E
A	O	X	O	C	A	I	N	S	S
N	O	I	T	A	T	P	M	E	T
N	B	V	E	N	R	Y	N	X	E
I	R	O	A	M	A	S	N	Y	R
V	C	M	T	I	U	N	N	F	U
E	E	O	H	U	O	T	M	V	T
R	N	X	U	R	E	Y	S	I	N
S	L	S	M	A	N	F	L	Y	E
A	T	O	N	U	T	R	X	L	V
R	U	O	M	U	H	I	A	A	D
Y	W	D	Y	O	F	I	M	K	A

TEMPTATION	ROMANTIC
SEXY	SENSUOUS
FUN	ADVENTURE
EXCITING	HUMOUR
TENTH	ANNIVERSARY

PLEASE TURN OVER FOR ENTRY DETAILS →

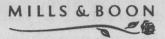

MILLS & BOON

HOW TO ENTER

10⁴ All the words listed overleaf below the wordsearch puzzle, are hidden in the grid. You can find them by reading the letters forward, backwards, up and down, or diagonally. When you find a word, circle it or put a line through it.

Don't forget to fill in your name and address in the space below then put this page in an envelope and post it today (you don't need a stamp). Closing date 31st May 1995.

Temptation Wordsearch,
FREEPOST,
P.O. Box 344,
Croydon,
Surrey
CR9 9EL

COMP395

Are you a Reader Service Subscriber?   Yes ☐   No ☐

Ms/Mrs/Miss/Mr _____

Address _____

_____

_____ Postcode _____